RETURN OF THE FOOTBALL FOSSILS

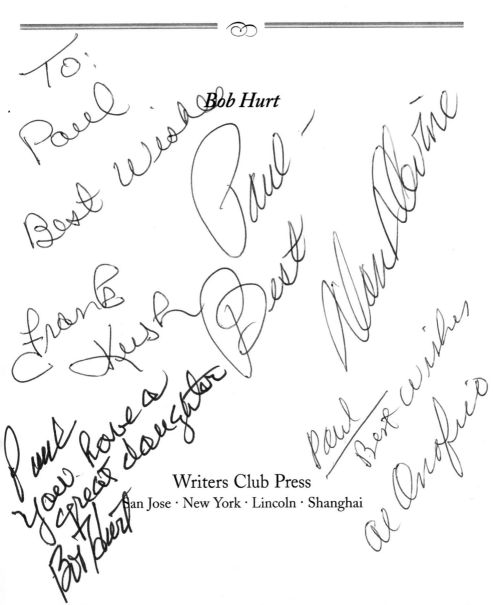

Bob Hurt

Writers Club Press
San Jose · New York · Lincoln · Shanghai

Return of the Football Fossils

Published by Writers Club Press
an imprint of iUniverse.com, Inc.

For information address:
iUniverse.com, Inc.
620 North 48th Street
Suite 201
Lincoln, NE 68504-3467
www.iuniverse.com

ISBN: 0-595-00078-9

Printed in the United States of America

PREFACE

Man can not live on golf alone, a truth I stumbled upon after only a few months of retirement. So what to do when not shanking and yipping my way around the links? How about writing a book? Breathes there an old-time newspaperman who has not dreamed this dream a time or two.

What has evolved is a somewhat unorthodox mixture of fact and fiction. The principal characters are real, living, breathing coaches. Their backgrounds are factual but the events into which I project them are fictional

The how-to-write books tell the would-be novelist to write about things he knows best. What I knew best was football coaches. Six of my favorites, all major college coaches, had settled, as I did, in metropolitan Phoenix,

My first thought was to mix the six into one composite fictional character. A problem developed. All of their personalities and approaches were different. Combining their interests and traits would produce one of the more enigmatic characters in fiction. Consider, please, the six ex-coaches:

—Soft-spoken Dan Devine (Arizona State, Missouri, Green Bay Packers, Notre Dame) was a master of nail-biting finishes but never received the recognition his accomplishments deserved.

—The exuberant Jack Mitchell (Arkansas, Kansas) was a throwback to his quarterbacking days at Oklahoma, where ball control and the kicking game were the keys to victory. He could throw the bull with the best of them.

—The solid, conservative Al Onofrio (Missouri) had a modest record but an amazing knack for engineering big upsets.

—Methodical, pains-taking Chuck Fairbanks (Oklahoma, New England Pats, Colorado) changed the thrust of his career by changing to a new offense at the most inopportune moment.

—Intense taskmaster Frank Kush (Arizona State, Baltimore/Indianapolis Colts) had a reputation as a strong disciplinarian which led to a weird situation in which he was honored, then dishonored, then honored again by Arizona State.

—Bright, innovative Darryl Rogers (Michigan State, Arizona State, Detroit Lions), was a good coach and a good person who was a victim of bad timing. He received inordinate criticism for one lousy tie.

Uniting the six on a mythical football staff gave me the opportunity to recall people and events that were high points in my nearly half century of sports writing. It also provided a platform to comment on the state of sports journalism and collegiate athletics,

I had fun writing it. I hope you have fun reading it.

—Bob Hurt

ACKNOWLEDGEMENTS

Profuse thanks to the six coaches who became the Football Fossils. They not only cooperated but also offered much encouragement. Good Conduct medals go to my personal editors, Jay Simon and Ellen Smith, for their patience with my shortcomings.

CHAPTER 1

Balmy is the operative word…

Balmy accurately describes this warm December evening in Orlando, Florida.

But balmy also is slang for being mildly crazy. In that connotation, it fit perfectly the behavior of the brash, young football team from Southwestern State, an emerging gridiron power from Phoenix, Arizona. It was to play its most important game ever on this balmy night in Florida. Scheduled to start within the hour was the Citrus Bowl.

Matched, or mis-matched in the opinion of many experts, were Southwestern and the University of Southern California. The USC Trojans had a larger-than-life-size football reputation. Southwestern had none, except that it had upset three of the bigger bigwigs in college football this season.

In public eyes, USC was Goliath and Southwestern a David without a slingshot.

USC has a superiority complex. The Trojans felt put upon about being in the Citrus Bowl. They had been counting on a better bowl and a better foe. Those hopes were dashed in the season's last scheduled game when they suffered their first loss of the season, being upset by arch rival UCLA.

Still, the Trojans were rated sixth nationally and thought they deserved a better bowl opponent than the upstart from Arizona.

It was to tweak the upturned nose of the haughty Trojans that Southwestern switched to unlikely and completely inappropriate attire for their warm-up an hour prior to kickoff. The stunt also served to loosen up the Rattlers, obviously somewhat awed by USC.

This contest was billed as "A Game of the Ages for the Aged." Obviously an exaggeration. It sounded like something whomped up by Don King, the Brillo-headed fight promoter. But, it was, as advertised, for the aged but hardly qualified as a game of the ages.

To reach this point, the Rattlers jumped more obstacles than an Olympic hurdler. The last and most formidable step was convincing the NCAA, the smug and stuffy ruler of collegiate athletics, to drop the ban on post-season competition placed on Southwestern after a mid-season cyber-cheating scandal. The leverage to pry Southwestern off probation was to turn the Citrus Bowl into a charity game for senior citizens.

It was a natural. Florida, California and Arizona lead the nation in retirees. The Disney Corp., with a strong presence in both California and Florida, tossed $14 million into the charity pot. Southwestern had produced instant senior citizen icons when it named six retired coaches to coach by committee through the last half of the season.

What a motley crew this was. Never has a college staff had more wrinkles or scars. One of the coaches had two knee operations, another had heart surgery, a third had back surgery and a fourth suffered with a serious prostate problem. The coaches needed a team doctor more than the team did.

At the first press conference in Orlando, the Southwestern staff sat behind a folding banquet table, fronted by a television station banner. In deference to their equal status, all six had microphones of their own.

The first question came from a veteran writer, a wiseass if there ever was one. He stood and let his gaze travel methodically from one coach to another. Then he posed the question:

"What is this? God's little waiting room?"

Cruel? Certainly. But not without some justification. This was the oldest staff ever assembled. It also may have been the best. It included two Hall of Fame inductees in Dan Devine and Frank Kush. Four of the staff members had been head coaches in the NFL—Devine, Kush, Darryl Rogers and Chuck Fairbanks. The other two, Jack Mitchell and Al Onofrio, had coached major college teams.

Coaching by committee supposedly is a course fraught with peril. The Chicago Cubs once tried it and discarded it.

But it was no problem for this group, which came to be called the Football Fossils. No one was jealous. No one worried about climbing the coaching ladder. There was no position to protect. This was the end of the line.

And what a way to go. The old war-horses were out of the pasture and back in a profession they dearly loved and sorely missed. And, best of all, they were beholden to no one. They could thumb noses at alums, tell off smart-aleck players and ignore obnoxious reporters.

Instead of an enemy, age became an ally to the Fossils. They kept delving into memory banks for trick plays, which became the staple for the Rattlers. Also, old strategy and stirring speeches used at an earlier time were recycled.

These six took Southwestern on a hell of a nostalgic rollercoaster ride, with sharp twists and breath-taking ups and downs.

But we get ahead of ourselves. Let's fast reverse five years to when it all started.

• • •

Southwestern State opened its doors then. And figuratively knocking at that door they found Boots Anderson. He wanted to coach football at the new institution. And he did. Damned well. Which was why Southwestern became, in infancy, a budding football factory.

The running start wasn't all because of Boots. The Valley of the Sun, which is Phoenix plus its suburbs, had a fine community college system which became a veritable assembly line producing good Southwestern football players. Plus, it was a snap to recruit out-of-staters after exposing them to the great Arizona weather and Southwestern's reputation as a party school.

But, mainly it was Boots. He put it all together. And he danged near tore it all apart with a few lies and an attempted cover up. Someone said he should have had an oval office.

Boots' name was not Boots. He was christened Socrates Homer Anderson. The name lasted only long enough to start a lot of fights, which Boots won. He was a tough kid, Boots was. He also was brash and boisterous and rowdy.

Boots came off a scrubby cattle ranch in southeastern Arizona. It was open range. Cattle could wander anywhere they wanted to wander. So could Boots. He wandered up to Tempe, where he walked on at Arizona State University in 1958.

Actually he came to ASU not afoot but in a battered Ford pickup truck. A walk-on has nothing to do with transportation. A walk-on, in athletic parlance, is a youngster who comes out for a team without benefit of a scholarship or other visible means of support.

According to legend, Boots wandered unannounced into the office of football coach Frank Kush, a tough guy who knew tough when he saw it.

"Mr. Kush, my name is Boots, and I am going to be a good football player. I stand 6-feet-4, weigh 230 pounds, run the 40-yard dash in 4.5 seconds, can high jump 6 feet 5 and have an A-minus average in school."

Kush withheld a smile and said, "Sounds awfully good, son. Too good. Don't you have any drawbacks?"

"Well," drawled Boots, "I do sometimes lie a little."

Now, that's an old story, used by dozens of coaches in banquet speeches. So no one could vouch for Boots actually saying those things, but it sounds like something he might say.

Boots, like many coaches, coached by rote, relying more on memory than ingenuity. Boots had apprenticed under some good coaches. Plus, he made it a point to hear the top men in the profession at clinics. In a given situation, then, he could tap his memory bank for a play, a piece of strategy, or an inspirational comment.

By the same token, Boots' public appearances generally were spiced with a quip or an anecdote plagiarized from another coach. Stealing such things from colleagues is a misdemeanor hardly worth a frown in coaching, a copy-cat profession.

Boots started practicing mimicking football coaching greats early on. His roommate at ASU, Horace Hackney, tells how Boots spent hours in front of a mirror imitating his idols. One minute he was a growling Kush, the next an erudite Joe Paterno and then a mean Bear Bryant.

Boots' favorite was Nebraska's late, great Bob Devaney, who combined toughness with a delightful Irish sense of humor. Devaney's canned chatter wowed 'em on the mashed-potato circuit. Samples:

"Told my wife her socks were wrinkled, and she wasn't wearing any.

"We had this skinny kid at fullback. Weighed 150, was 6–4. When he drank a strawberry pop he looked like a thermometer. Best thing about him was he fit the holes our linemen made."

"Went on a two-week diet. Lost 14 days."

"Went to Vegas. Lost 14 cents in a stamp machine."

Boots, like Devaney, was something of a rogue. They never saw a party they didn't like. Both were members in good standing of the dawn patrol. It showed. Beneath Boots' bushy brows were eyes with more red lines than a road map. His face was weathered, furrowed. Only W. C. Fields would have liked his bulbous nose.

Boots was only mediocre as a player, but now is listed as an all-conference player. Amazing, isn't it? The older we get the better we were.

Boots coached in high school for two years in southern Arizona, put in short stints as an assistant at three different universities and was head coach at two different junior colleges. He was the first applicant at Southwestern. He campaigned for the job. He got it, probably by lying a little.

Boots wore his Levis low, a substantial stomach overflowing his big, silver belt buckle. Boots always wore boots. He had dress boots and work boots. He had boots skinned off alligators and lizards. He had cleated boots for golf, patent leather boots for dancing.

He fit right in at Southwestern State, originally a satellite of Arizona State University. The satellite grew so rapidly that the Board of Regents, pressured by pupils, politicians and professors, blessed the erstwhile satellite five years ago with independent status and a new name. What had been ASU West became Southwestern State. A nickname, the Rattlers, was added by vote of the student body. Several smart aleck students submitted a write-in vote for "Artichokes," although well aware that this edible nickname had been taken by Scottsdale Community College.

Southwestern was an independent, with no conference affiliation, but was not entirely independent of Arizona State University. Southwestern remained tied to ASU by several facilities, which the Regents decreed the two should share in the interest of economy. One such shared facility was a football stadium seating 73,000.

This upscale stadium was nestled between two buttes and its parking extended to the new Town Lake on the north. The stadium was no stranger to capacity crowds. The arena had hosted the Super Bowl and three national collegiate championship games.

The stadium had been remodeled to accommodate two tenants in 1988. ASU dressed in the basement of a athletic office building which held up the south end of the stadium. Two more teams were nicely accommodated in a new building, located some 100 yards north of the north endzone.

It included locker rooms for two teams and a mini auditorium. That had been added to attract the Arizona Cardinals of the NFL. The Cards soon defected to a stadium of their own, leaving ASU with two vacant locker rooms, for which there was little demand.

Sun Devil stadium, with double decked skyboxes and a huge press box, gave Southwestern the credibility to attract decent foes. The Rattlers became an even more desirable opponent because they were willing to travel. So, they had a better schedule than team. Until last year.

In his fourth season, Boots' team won seven games, more than the other three years combined, and went to the Bluebonnet bowl as a result.

Boots' idol, as mentioned, was the late Bob Devaney, whose philosophy was summed up with his oft-used statement: "I want a team good enough to be investigated but not good enough to go on probation."

Boots seconded this notion. He was caught fudging on rules ever so often. He sloughed off such stuff. "Everybody does it," he told the school president.

So it was inevitable that Boots eventually would get caught in a serious violation. Had he 'fessed up in the grade-changing scandal, he might have escaped with a hand-slapping. But he tried to lie his way out of trouble. The result was that he and his staff all were ousted, leaving Southwestern with six games to play and no coaches.

The solution to this mid-season crisis? Well, that's where the Football Fossils came in.

CHAPTER 2

It becomes of some importance to know me, since it is through my eyes the story is told. I had been a pretty good sportswriter for 45 years. Friends were stunned when I left sportswriting.

Why quit sportswriting? Not because sportswriters are underpaid, although they are. But I never considered what I did was work. What others pay to get into, I got paid to attend. It was a great life for a guy who loves sports, but who could not play them.

I am short, but slow and uncoordinated. I was the equivalent of a gutter ball, a blocked kick or a double fault. In football, I got one letter. It said bring back the equipment.

Be advised that my nickname is "Bull," which is something I frequently throw. I prefer to think the nickname is only a derivation of my last name. I am Raymond Bullington.

Sportswriting was fun, but the fun faded. Sports have changed more than I have. Best contests now are in the courts, or over the negotiating table.

And the trend toward confrontational journalism has turned unqualified kids into critics. That was part of why I hung 'em up. But the big thing was that I wanted to come out of the closet as a sports fan. Sportswriters, good ones at least, strive to be neutral. Decorum requires writers to be objective. This means any form of emotional approval or dis-approval is barred from press boxes.

Once, movie star Gordon MacRae, after singing the National Anthem at a Nebraska game, grabbed a spot in the press box to watch the game. He was appalled at the utter silence in the press box as the game grew closer. When the Huskers mounted what was to be the winning drive, he stood and shouted, "What's wrong with you people? Why aren't you cheering?"

A press box steward whispered in the singer's ear, explaining that the press box was a working area and that those in it were required to refrain from cheering or jeering. The singer left with a red face.

Only once can I recall sportswriters losing it in a press box. Well, it wasn't exactly a press box. It was the top two rows of a tiny high school gym in Lake Placid, N. Y. As the USA hockey team did the unbelievable, beating Russia in the 1980 Winter Olympics, representatives of the New York Times, The Chicago Tribune, the San Francisco Chronicle and others stood clapping and shouting—like so many well lubricated Cubs' fans.

So I sought escape, a life in which I could at least privately root for the home team and rub elbows with coaches and athletes without being accused of being a "homer." I became Sports Information Director (SID) at Southwestern State in the same season the Fossils arrived.

Envisioned was a pleasant, quiet way to phase out. It was anything but.

A secretary and private office came with the job. That wowed me. Reporters rarely have either. No sooner was I ensconced in a swivel chair than my first visitor arrived. He was short but firm and fully packed. Muscles rippled atop muscles.

Ed Glavin was the school's veteran wrestling coach. I was genuinely happy to greet him as my first official visitor. Ed was a nice, sweet old guy with old-fashioned values. At least, I had written such things about him only a month earlier in the newspaper.

I thought he had come to welcome me, but such niceties quickly were put aside.

"You're supposed to be our new spin doctor," he said, volume growing with each word. I nodded, even though he was going to proceed with or without an answer. His radiator was on the verge of boiling over.

"You're paid big money to keep this kind of stuff out of the paper," he said, tossing a clipping to me. "I tell this kid reporter that we don't do anything special. . don't take any extreme measures to help our wrestlers make weight. And this is what I get."

The headline on the article jumped out at me, "Weighty Wrestling Problem Poses Death Threat."

The kid reporter had done a decent job with his story. It was nothing new. Every newspaper, at least once a year, criticizes a college wrestling team for the torture chamber tactics wrestlers must undergo to make their assigned weight level. It was not the story so much as the headline that got Glaven's juices flowing.

"The reporter doesn't write the headlines," I explained patiently. "Another guy, working on the desk, does that. And he basically writes to fit the space."

That went over like a pregnant pole-vaulter.

"Why would they let a person I've never met write the headline? He doesn't come to practice or matches, doesn't come to press conferences. And most people don't read anything but the headline."

I raised the white flag, taking the coward's way out. "You're right, coach. I'll talk to them."

Next up was football coach Boots Anderson. He called, ordering me to report to the worn carpet in front of his oversized mahogany desk. The furrows on his face had deepened and reddened. It was obvious this was not a social call.

"Hell, this newspaper is reporting our injuries," he said, waving said periodical in my face.

"Was it accurate?"

"Your freaking ass it was. That's what makes it so bad. Since when did our newspapers switch sides? Since when did they think it was their duty to aid and abet the enemy? You think that won't help them prepare? Should we ditto all our plays and send them to the paper with a copy to every team on the schedule?"

I explained, in a somewhat quivering voice, that complete reporting of injuries is considered only fair to the reading public. Bookies and other teams have the information. It's the public that is screwed by being kept in the dark. The NFL, he was told, feels strongly on the subject. It demands quick and accurate injury reports. Violators face stiff fines.

"OK, we'll just close practice to those reporters," said the coach. "Hell, they'd go to a wedding and write about the bride's ugly dress."

Welcome, Bull, to intercollegiate athletics.

The sports information director (SID) does not punch a time clock. Southwestern has 22 sports. All require attention. No longer can he concentrate on just revenue sports. The information department is required to have a representative at every event. I have two assistants and two student assistants, who are stretched to cover 500 events a year.

The SID needs to be an administrator, writer, spin doctor and advisor. He must support coaching decisions with which he does not agree. He must soothe both angry coaches and angry writers. He must listen to the public and the administrators. He's the straining rope in the middle of a tug of war.

CHAPTER 3

The thin line the SID walks was a stroll in the park compared to the rocky path encountered by the faculty representative, a largely unknown and grossly unappreciated force in collegiate athletics. Appointed by the president, this person must bridge the ever-widening gap between academe and athletics while at the same time making sense of the frequently senseless NCAA eligibility rules. It's a thankless job.

Coaches look on the faculty rep as an enemy from within while professors look on him as a turncoat selling out to athletic interests. To the athletic booster, he is another roadblock to be circumvented. To the athletic director, he is the final voice on NCAA rules.

In the case of Southwestern State, "he" was a she, although often referred to as "her." Meet Shirley Tate, full professor in the business school. I met her at a faculty party. While others in the athletic department were turned off by her decisions, I was turned on by her appearance. A raving beauty she wasn't. But everything seemed to go together so well. She had great legs, a nice smile and body to match. She was bronzed like a new penny, mute witness to many productive hours on the tennis courts.

Only flaw in her appearance was the bun into which her coal black hair was wound. It was wound so tightly it left her face contorted into a perpetual smile.

You've seen those movies in which the wallflower's conservative bun would be unraveled in the heat of passion, cascading strikingly down to the shoulders, and removing the last vestige of the staid professor. Such a striking transformation I could envision in Shirley.

Old goats need love, too. In my mind, I knew I was no Rex Harrison. But circumstances beyond my control had misled me into thinking I was something of a senior sex symbol.

I was 65 and dumpy and singularly ineffective as a Don Juan in my early years. Try to appreciate the sudden and heady change when I became a widower six years ago. Almost immediately, I was popular in the geriatric set, where women far outnumber men.

Sex, or the pursuit thereof, became a big part of my single life. Errol Flynn I wasn't. But it became important to try. I reacted for all the world like my stray tabby cat, Rudolph.

His front claws have been removed but Rudolph apparently does not know it. He keeps scratching the scratching pole with clawless paws. Sexually, I had been de-clawed—a fact which did not deter me from trying.

So, you can understand why the adrenaline flowed when I met Shirley Tate. She was 50-something and had been divorced 15 years earlier. She was too bright and too attractive to become involved with a broken-down sportswriter. Or was she?

I probably would not have had the guts to find out until I received this hunk of manna from heaven, arriving in the form of an executive order from the president's office. It pointed out that Shirley had been the victim of some rather unkind words in the public prints and asked if I would be willing to meet with her and offer a few public relations tips.

Would I ever.

• • •

There were no witches' brooms in the umbrella stand, as I had been warned to expect in Ms. Tate's modest office.

Reassuring. Maybe the other criticisms I had heard about her from the coaches and many of the moneyed alums were not deserved.

Shirley Tate, it must be stipulated, had this peculiar notion that athletes also should students be. That is, the student-athlete, as the NCAA prefers to call them, should have potential in the classroom as well as on the playing fields.

A series of adverse decisions on eligibility of athletes turned Shirley Tate into a favored whipping boy…er ah, whipping person…in the local press. Both media and fans viewed her as a major roadblock. The good programs had more cooperative faculty representatives, argued her detractors.

It is true, unfortunately, that success often starts with the ability to get fringe students into school. Sometimes it seems the less brains the athlete has the more likely he is to run faster, jump higher and hit harder.

So I entered her office all a-quiver, both in awe of her reputation but also titillated by her regal appearance and the opportunity to change her view of the student-athlete.

Before presenting myself, I had solicited advice from athletic department folks who had appeared before her earlier.

"Above all, don't call her 'little lady.'" said Boots Anderson, who had made that mistake.

"Don't try to bribe her with tickets and trips, " said Frazier Herman, assistant athletic director. He did and was scolded soundly.

"Independence is critical in this position," Shirley told Herman. "I can't be beholden to those in the athletic department because I have to call them as I see them."

On reflection, I was patronizing. I complimented her dress and hairdo. Could this be politically incorrect? A congressional act insists on equality between men and women in intercollegiate sports.

Shirley's problem with coaches and their supporters, I explained, was one of perception, which belabored the obvious.

"People think of you as a roadblock, not a starting block," I said.

She stifled a snicker, and patiently explained she was aware of her perception but insisted she had been assigned a difficult job and was not trying to win a Miss Congeniality contest.

An early-day Southwestern State president once announced his ambition of turning the university into a "Harvard of the West."

Gulp. Southwestern was a solid school, strong in many areas. But a Harvard it was not, nor ever would be. It served the blue-collared folks, the community college grads, and the commuters.

It was putting an unfair burden on the athletic department to expect the coaches to attract the top student who also happened to be an athlete. Good athletes with exceptional academic credentials would gravitate to a Stanford or a Duke or a Northwestern.

I quoted an anonymous Southwestern coach who had said, "If you're going to fly with the eagles, you had better schedule Harvard and Yale."

Tate bristled. With exaggerated patience, she explained her situation.

"I was appointed to this position with the charge to improve grade point averages and the graduation rate in the athletic department. And. absolutely no scandals. Those were my marching orders. That was part of the reason I took the job. The president assured me there would be no compromise."

No compromise? That promise lasted about as long as it took to make it.

Dr. Justin White had recently moved from a small, scholarly school in Iowa to become president at Southwestern. He had no appreciation of the pressures which come with big-time football. So, he promised Shirley he would not compromise to assist the football program. The "no compromise' edict was made in good faith but with absolutely no chance of fulfilling it.

Two months later, Tate ruled a star tailback ineligible, refusing to accept his junior college credits. He had not followed guidelines required of all students, she ruled.

The press, coaches and alums took turns lampooning Tate as a "hard hearted school marm unconcerned with the school's best interests."

So in her third month on the job, Tate wound up on the president's carpet along with the athletic director, Harrison Johnston. Dr. White put the evil eye on his faculty rep and said,

"I think it would be in your best interests to reach a compromise on this issue."

Compromise translates to surrender.

The faculty senate heard about the "compromise" and unanimously voted Tate its support, in probably the only unanimous move it ever made.

No matter. Football is the tail which wags the animal. We should have listened when another college president, from Chicago, I think, said many years ago, "Football bears as much relationship to higher education as bullfighting does to agriculture."

It's not that coaches are a bunch of crooks. Indeed, most would rather be on the field coaching than in recruits' living rooms stretching both rules and ethical standards.

Coaches, endowed with colossal egos, feel they can out-coach anyone, given a level playing field. Alas, the level playing field is an impossible dream. The NCAA passes volumes of rules—but never one without a loophole the devious coach can find. College presidents and the majority of college coaches want cheating out of the game.

Face this: College athletics have grown too big for their own good. They have huge stadia, with huge mortgages. Even those edifices which are paid off require upward of $100,000 just to open for a game. Coaching salaries also hit seven figures. Athletes' salaries? Who knows. Alums, who should know better, consider football the rallying point. Woe be to the president who starts a capital fund drive without a winning football team.

"Football is such a big business now you couldn't get along without it," said Tate. "To me, that is the ethical dilemma. It's a web. A lot of time I come out of one of those meetings and want to take a shower."

Funny, I went to sway Tate and ended up being swayed by her.

Back to the mission: How to put a new spin on the much-maligned faculty rep. She was willing to cooperate.

"First, if you want to change the public perception of you," I said, "You have to mingle with the public. How about letting me take you to Saturday's football game. I'll introduce you to some bigwigs and writers. It can't hurt.

"And if you don't want a freebie ticket, we'll let you buy one."

CHAPTER 4

It is a no-no for the Sports Information director to desert the press box on game days. But President White has not been around long enough to be influenced by tradition. So, he insisted I escort Ms. Tate to the next football game.

Not that I put up great resistance, understand.

So, there we were, Shirley and Bull in the stands with the plebeians watching a favored Southwestern team get its tail kicked by New Mexico State, hardly acceptable demeanor for a bowl team.

It was a rare day off for me. Except there was little joy in it. As the questions flowed from Shirley's ever-moving lips I squirmed down in my grandstand seat and edged away from her.

"It's a nice park," she said, looking down on the patch of greensward surrounded by riotous partisans. "But why would they disfigure it by painting all those white lines and driving posts into it?

"And why are those convicts in stripes running around down there."

"Well, if they're game officials, why do they have to keep huddling to make a decision."

"Why is the ball oblong. Aren't other sports played with round balls?"

"Why is it so much harder to make a touchdown than a first down."

"Why do they call him the tight end? Is he inebriated or stingy? Why do they have one quarterback when they play four quarters? And why does it take four quarters to consume one fifth?"

"Why do they keep limping off the field and then running back on. Do they bust the strings in those corsets or what?"

The crowd was loud, and quickly growing more hostile, but Shirley's voice rose above it all. Or so it seemed to me.

Finally, the burly guy on her left leaned over. I feared violence. But he said, "Hey, honey, want a drink?"

"Why yes," she said sweetly. "A big orange, please."

That should have silenced him, but did not. As Southwestern's deficit grew so did his ire. It was directed primarily at the Southwestern cornerback.

After a full quarter of hearing him berate the cornerback profanely and viciously, Shirley had all she could take. She turned, grabbed the burly one by the front of his shirt and twisted him around so they were face to angry face.

"Listen, you lummox," she shouted above the crowd noise. "Anybody who knows football knows they are in Cover Two. That's double coverage, mister. When the split end goes deep and wide the cornerback checks him off to the safety. It's the safety who's screwing up."

I gulped. What she said was correct. But how could this gridiron dunce be transformed before my very eyes into a knowledgeable football fan?

Some of her monologue sounded familiar. I had been searching my mind. Where had I heard this before? Finally a light flashed on in my mind. There was an old Andy Griffith record in which he played the role of a hick seeing his first football game.

I turned to Shirley and grinned. "Hey, that's a helluva show. But it sounds a heck of a lot like that old Andy Griffith record. You sound like a hick one minute and Knute Rockne the next. What gives?"

"Funny you should say that," she said, her face twisting into impish grin. She knew she had taken me in.

"Last night I got down that old Andy Griffith football classic recording, and you're right, I stole a few lines from it. Rockne I am not. But I also am not the total idiot everyone in the athletic department thinks I am. My dad was a high school coach for 30 years. My two brothers both played football. I coached a Pop Warner team through two seasons myself."

A flash of recognition crossed the burly one's face. "You're the faculty representative, aren't you? You're the one ruining our program. You're Shirley Tate. I saw your picture in the paper the other day throwing darts at pictures of the coaches."

"Guilty as charged," she smiled. "Except that was a cartoon, not a picture."

"Pleasure to meet you, ma'm. Could I have your autograph."

She sighed, signed and then turned down an invitation to join the burly one at a post-game tailgate party.

She had charmed one detractor, but I did not dare chance another confrontation and suggested we adjourn to the press box.

En route I gave her a quick tour of the skyboxes. A total of 59 of these plush boxes were erected in two stories atop the west stands. These boxes came with bars, snacks, johns and hot and cold running water. They were peddled to corporations at an average of $10,000 a year.

The boxes turn me off. Oh, I visited them at half times to rub elbows with the big givers and to indulge in macadamia nut cookies and a vodka-tonic. But I wouldn't want to see a game from the box. This was an isolation booth. Patrons were locked away from the noise, the bands and the excitement which makes football fun.

The press box is a magnificent work place stretching out atop the second deck between the 10-yard lines. It is 122 feet above the field, which requires its denizens to have good binoculars or good imagination or both.

Radio and TV booths, each with three work levels, are at the north end. The two-tiered area for print media is at the south. Telephones are available at each location. They are wired for the latest in laptop computers. Behind them was a huge press lounge, where dinners were served and snacks were always available.

Shirley's lower jaw dropped at the expanse of it. "You mean we have this and it is used less than a dozen times a year?"

I went into a spiel about how the school and the state are viewed by the nation through this glass-enclosed edifice. This was first class. Ergo, the state was first class. Besides, a sellout brought in more than $2 million. Also, pros had played here. So did rock bands.

The explanation did little to remove the scowl from Shirley's face. Off quickly to Plan B. As chance would have it, the two of us were approached at this moment by Bill "Scoop' Simon, the most respected columnist in the state and a guy who had ridiculed Shirley and her decisions endlessly.

Shirley grimaced. Bill looked sheepish. They had not met but she recognized him from the picture atop his column. I performed the introductions, found coffee and seats in the press lounge. After which I showed no courage whatsoever. I suggested they talk and hastily retreated. I can't stand the sight of blood. But, hell, Shirley had survived the guy in the stands. Maybe she could survive Scoop. Either way, I badly needed a respite. I went to check on my troops who keep the statistics. Shirley and Scoop sat at a table already occupied by three other veteran reporters who later told me what happened.

As they sat, Scoop's cellphone rang. Scoop pulled the phone from his hip pocket and placed it against Shirley's ear.

"Please answer this for me," he said to Shirley. The others shook heads in disbelief. Scoop was being crude and condescending. But Shirley submitted meekly.

"Hello," she said, and listened to the caller.

"Yes, he is here" she said nicely, "But he can't come to the phone. He's not dressed."

The table exploded in guffaws and hearty leg slapping, which quickly rubbed the frown off Scoop's face. His colleagues thought it was great. Scoop had to think so, too, or lose face.

Thus the ice was broken. Shirley and Scoop quickly shifted into easy conversation.

I watched them from the glass enclosed cubicle where statisticians do their thing and saw they had no trouble finding conversational fodder. Sometimes, the conversation seemed a bit animated but not angry. By the time I returned, the second half had started but neither party felt inclined to end the conversation.

Bill, a snake in the public prints, was charmed by the wit and logic to which he had been exposed, a fact validated by his first words.

"I'm certainly glad Shirley and I did not meet earlier. It would have ruined a hell of a lot of columns for me.

"Do you realize no member of the local media has ever talked to her? Well, no one has. If you feature yourself a PR man, you will remedy that. Shirley comes through great one on one. Let her meet the press over coffee and cookies, nothing formal, just an opportunity to state her position and answer questions. You may not go along with her positions, but you'll have a lot better idea of why she did what she did."

CHAPTER 5

Sportswriters are a compatible group. Sometimes too compatible. The game they play often resembles follow the leader. Let one guy pick up a good quote or a fresh angle and everyone else follows his lead. Hell, sharing has gone high tech. Networks have been established. Selected scribes may huddle with a dozen other scribes once weekly over long-distance lines or on the world wide web.

Plagiarism running wild? No. We just view it as appropriate research. Never mind that it helps get a journalist to the golf course earlier.

This explains why we were all gathered in a steamy, basement mini-auditorium for Shirley Tate's first full-fledged press conference. Most journalists gathered there were following the lead of Scoop Simon, who had written a good piece about Tate, and the woes of being a faculty rep. Scoop refused to retreat from his earlier criticism of Tate but did admit she might have some legitimate points.

A refreshing idea, this, good enough in this copy-cat atmosphere to bring out many writers and electronic guys for the press conference.

Arizonians admit to 100-degree temperatures, but inevitably add, "It is a dry heat." Put an asterisk on that footnote. The heat is dry except between mid July and early October. That is the monsoon time, the time moist air is pushed up from Mexico.

Residents are forced to live beneath their air conditioners. Without said air conditioners, the Phoenix area would have been inhabited only by gila monsters and rattlesnakes instead of overweight, pale-faced, Bermuda-shorted tourists.

Some 50 members of the press were shoe-horned into the small basement room beneath the athletic business building to quiz Shirley. With this mob, plus the blinding lights sprouting from five television cameras, the air conditioner was fighting a losing battle. Heat and sweat tended to make the inhabitants a little testy.

Q—What was your introduction to Southwestern athletics?

Tate—"The first day I went to my office I was handed SAT (Scholastic Aptitude Test) scores for athletes. They ran about 500. I looked at them and said, 'Okay, is that for the verbal or math part? My secretary burst out laughing, and said, 'That's the total score.'"

Q—So what did you do?

Tate—"Procedures were an unholy mess. Everyone waited until the last minute to submit transcripts. I said, Okay, we can fix that. They won't practice until they get the documents in."

Q—How long did that last?

Tate—"Just long enough for the president to tell me I should cooperate. So I started going to the athletic department staff meetings. It just turned into perfunctory meetings when I arrived. Nothing of any substance was discussed."

I gulped and tried to grab the microphone. This was not the kind of publicity I was hired to produce. Shirley laughed at my effort, and waved me off. The questions continued.

Q—But the football people treat you like a lady, right?

Tate—"Yeah, right. The coach kept calling me "Little Lady." It was blatant. Some people, who don't know about being politically correct, use that as a term of endearment. I could endure that. But the coach was doing it on purpose, using it as a bargaining chip."

Q—Did you feel the true academic shortcomings in athletics were being hidden?

Tate—"Sure. It was appalling to see some of those youngsters being recruited. My answer was to release to the press the report on cumulative grades of athletes. They had never been published before. The coaches were up in arms but the regents' policy required it. The president didn't say much but he obviously was not happy about it."

Q—Ruling on eligibility problems can be touchy. Right?

Tate—"Yes, every kid with an eligibility problem was one who, I was told by the coaches, could make the difference between winning and losing. The head coaches, I became convinced, spend most of their time finding ways to circumvent the NCAA rules."

Q—Aren't eligibility matters validated by transcripts and other written documents?

Tate—"But so much of the paper work was bogus. Sometimes you just wished that, if they were going to cheat, they would be smarter about it. We had one kid taking a test for another kid. They were from different races.

"I've seen white-out to alter notes on a yellow legal pad.

"Typically, the at-risk student-athlete would submit pieces of paper to me and claim the numbers were test scores. We required that all such evidence be verified. One person changed the name on a transcript and tried to pass it off as his. But he forgot to change the social security number."

Q—So, these guys didn't make the grade even at cheating. Surely, you've had some clever bogus papers?

Tate—"We've had documents show up that were completely opposite to what you'd expect. I can't prove it, but I think they got computer hackers to change the transcripts—improving the grades or. . Well, it was remarkable how many instances we found where a two-hour course had, without explanation, become a five-hour course. And there also were times when grades from the community colleges were changed. I always had one questionable pile of papers on my desk."

Q—But if these guys were supposed to be dumb how could they infiltrate a school's computer and change records?

Tate—"You have to realize there are a lot of highly skilled computer technicians around a college. The hackers see doing something like this as a challenge.

"And, a couple of times I've been suspicious of staff people being involved."

Whoa, my mind told me. As a PR guy, I was supposed to suppress such stuff, not disseminate it. I grabbed the mike and said, "Well, that's all we have time for. That was the last question."

But reporters already were streaking for phones. This was the stuff from which headlines were made. A sampling: IS THE MODEM THE MODERN WAY TO VICTORY? THE CUTTING EDGE: CYBERCHEATS? WINNING FORMULA: BLOCK, TACKLE AND HACK

Another point, not raised in the articles, was this: Does the sports information director, your old friend Bull Bullington, start looking for new job?

CHAPTER 6

The irony of the situation delighted editorial writers. Here, the computer, which has become such a valuable educational tool, was being used to compromise the integrity of an educational institution.

Transcript tampering, however, was not the first time nor will it be the last time cyberspace is misused in academic circles.

Need a term paper or an essay? Just dial up "cyberfratfile" on the web, pick a subject, and press "print." No cost. Other web sites offer papers for fees ranging from $20 to $100.

Internet athletic scouting services feed on colleges and the athletes. Sportspics has 950 colleges as clients. More than 3,000 prep prospects paid $69 apiece to be listed last year on another service, the Online Sports Network.

Still, the news media was startled by Southwest's alleged computer transcript tampering. Good high-tech stuff there. Seasoned reporters were familiar with normal forms of athletic misconduct—passing car keys under table or providing cushy jobs for relatives or inordinate salaries for summer employment. But who, pray tell, would have thought cyberspace would open a backdoor to college athletics?

Jaded journalists jumped to attention. The allegations prompted inordinate press coverage. Half of the front page of The Arizona Republic, the state's leading newspaper, was devoted to the budding scandal. Suburban papers followed suit. Radio talk shows and television stations scrambled for expert witnesses.

No further impetus was needed but Southwestern's august athletic director, Harrison Johnston, added oil to the fire. Said he, "There is absolutely no way our computer system could have been breached in the manner suggested."

Talk show telephones were jammed by hackers eager to ridicule Johnston. They asked: If hackers could invade the department of defense, the CIA, Los Alamos, AT&T and the FBI, as they have, why would Southwestern's system be impregnable?

The Associated Press reported that hackers infiltrate Pentagon computers 160,000 times a year.

Said the commissioner of the Pacific Ten conference, David Snider: "Only the most naive would presume their computer could not be cracked. Now, that's off the record, isn't it."

Said a high-ranking official in the NCAA: "I could not comment on such a statement. But if you'll promise not to attribute it to me I can tell you we now are investigating two cases in which computer fraud is suspected in altering grades."

Few are aware of the highwaymen on the information highway. The public pictures the hacker as being some egghead kid pulling pranks to feed his ego. But dark-side hacking is reaching epidemic proportions. The FBI estimates that losses in computer fraud annually range between $500 million and $5 billion.

The only absolutely secure computer, writes noted hacker tracker Tsutomu Shimomura, was one unplugged and locked in a safe.

The Arizona Republic took its questions to a leading national expert on computer crimes in its own backyard:

Could it happen? Is it plausible to consider grades being changed by computer?

"Oh sure," said Gail Thackeray, deputy county attorney who conducts training classes on computer security nationally. "It already has happened. It was in our community college system. A bright youngster invaded the system from Phoenix College and changed grades at Mesa Community College.

"The kid was not in it for the money. He was in it to show off. It happens all the time. In this case, Phoenix College had a good computer security man. He caught the youngster earlier and a dean had lectured the youngster about never doing it again. "

Could it happen even in a large university like, say, Southwestern State?

"Very easily," Thackeray continued. "We had a case where a young man came out of the military and invaded about 40 of Arizona State's computers. He had control of passwords that gave him access to everything."

Thackeray gained national recognition as one of four most instrumental in Operation Sundevil. Thackeray, then with the Arizona Attorney General's organized crime division, helped establish a sting operation on those suspected of operating illegal bulletin boards.

Secret Service and FBI officers were among 150 agents who struck with 27 search warrants in 12 different cities. Attention was focused on the growing problem, which, heretofore largely was overlooked by the press.

Expert that she was, Thackeray had pinpointed the Achilles heel of hackers. The nerds like to show off. Eager to brag, they jammed talk show switchboards. "Hell," said one, "You'd have to be awful dumb to think it has not been done before. There are at least 200 hackers in the Phoenix area who could hack into the Southwestern system. On the average, it would take them about 20 minutes."

Harrison Johnston had receded into the background after his first statement but could not allow the hacker's boast to stand unchallenged.

"Nonsense," he snorted at the hacker's break-in claims.

Whereupon, the local hacker involved substantiated his contention by breaking into the Southwestern computer and changing Johnston's resume. The AD became 21 years of age instead of 54. His weight was changed from 210 to 118.

Apprised of the changes by a talk show host, Johnston checked his computer and, one suspects, gulped. He was not heard from again on the subject.

CHAPTER 7

And the walls came tumbling down, quickly and neatly. It was not an explosion as much as a implosion. The Southwestern football program, having crumbled from within, was left in shambles.

The final nail in the coffin came from another talk show. It pains me to credit a talk show. I don't put much credence in talk shows and/or letters to the editor. Such forums are used, too often, by the sports lunatic fringe. It irritates me when a newspaper, which has well-trained and well-educated experts in its midst, leans on anonymous and often irrational outsiders for opinions.

The call to the talk show came at 11:45 p.m. The caller lisped and talked softly but his message came in loud and clear. The anonymous caller identified himself by his electronic handle, The Galloping Ghost. I shuddered. Red Grange this kid was not. But the Ghost's first words grabbed my attention:

"I am the guy who the Southwestern coach bribed to change the grades of some of his academically challenged players."

Academically challenged? He giggled at his choice of words.

The talk show host, showing an economy of words uncommon in his business, said: "Please just tell us how the coach contacted you, how he bribed you and how you invaded the Southwestern computer?

The Ghost obviously was proud of his computer skills. His ego needed feeding.

"Well, it was late last summer. I was having a brew one night with some friends at Campus Corner. I was telling them, like, how I had hacked into the academic records section and had almost instantly become a Phi Beta Kappa. I offered to pump up their grades for a fee.

"I was leaving when an elderly gentleman, like, tugged on my shirt and asked if he could talk to me. He, I found out, was Boots Anderson, the Southwestern football coach. He said he had been in the booth behind me and had heard me explain how to fix up grades.

"Well," he said to me, "'I've got a couple of players who need help. A running back and a punter. Great boys. Fine athletes. They aren't going to be eligible. And Southwestern needs them. It might be the difference between a .500 year and going to a bowl. If you care anything about your university, you'll help.'"

"I told him I didn't care if Southwestern ever won another game or not. But that I did have a girl friend that liked the game and could use a couple of tickets on the 50-yard line to impress her.

"So, the coach, he said to me, 'You've got it son. And just for good measure, I'll let you and the girl ride the team plane to Indiana, our first road game.' So, I told him I'd do it."

The talk show host asked how he cracked the system.

The Ghost returned to his monologue. "That was not difficult. There's a new program being passed around the underground called a 'sniffer.' You can put it in a computer and the owner never knows its there. But it, like, picks up all the passwords and user names. You just hack back into the computer, get the info and go to work. With that stuff, I like infiltrated the system administrator's file, and from there to the registrar.

"But I probably could have worked it out another way because the coach let me use his computer. We got into the office at midnight. I remember the night, because it was my birthday, August 14. It's, like, a breeze. We change the running back's two-hour course into a five-hour course. On the other guy, the punter, we turn an F into a C and he's eligible. Probably didn't take over 20 minutes."

With that, the hacker hung up. But the story was not forgotten. The station wouldn't permit that. It replayed the tape every hour on the hour for two days, and made it available to all other media in the area.

Response to the interview? Well, Johnston was in his shell. The president, Dr. Justin White, had retreated into his no-comment stance.

And me, Bull Bullington, fledgling SID? Well, I fell back on the old cliché, "We're looking into it."

The problem in a serious investigation was that Boots had a lot of friends and followers. You had to like what he had done with the football program. And if he bent the rules? Everybody does it, his loyalists insisted.

That is always the excuse for breaching NCAA rules.

Into this void rode an unlikely wannabe hero. Dr. Percival N. Pickens. Pickens had been a vice president at Southwestern for two years. He wanted more, if you judge from the stilettos he left lodged in some colleagues' backs. He had played football at Oklahoma. Fourth team defensive back. And he served as a dean of men there, until he was advised to start looking for a new job.

So, he saw Boots' problems as a ladder which, if handled properly, might be his route to a presidency at Southwestern or a comparable school. He ingratiated himself to Dr. White, God knows how. Perhaps he had intimidated White with his knowledge of football.

It was Pickens, then, who did what had to be done, even if not with altruistic motives. He privately launched an investigation starting with the school's computer security people. And he nosed around in the ticket department. And then he browbeat White into calling a meeting.

Boots declined the invitation until told his job hung in the balance. Johnston pleaded illness. So I was dispatched to represent the athletic department. As the link between athletics and academe, Shirley Tate attended.

Say this for Pickens, he came prepared. He had interviewed a Wilbur Jennings, AKA the Galloping Ghost, promising immunity and anonymity for his cooperation. Facts, as recited on the talk show, were validated, he said.

"Who are you going to believe, me or this pimply-faced kid?" said an angry Boots.

"I intend to believe evidence," said Pickens coolly. "And we have more."

Thereupon, Pickens presented first a document from the ticket office attesting that in late August, two season tickets on the 50-yard line had been sent to a Wilbur Jennings. Further research showed that Jennings and a friend were among the guests on the team plane going to Indiana.

Then, the university computer security officer was called. He testified that he had dug deeply into the university computer hard drive where deleted files could be restored. Most entries followed a predictable pattern, being sent by the same people during working hours. Except for one. There had been an invasion on August 14 at 12:01 a.m. Electronic footprints led back to the coach's office.

"I don't have to take this crap," Boots blustered. "This is my team and this is my school and I don't deserve to be investigated. I've done too much for this school, and everybody knows it."

Say this for Justin White. When forced, he would take a stand, surprisingly a rather firm one.

"Be advised, Mr. Anderson," the president said, "That you are suspended as head coach pending further investigation. Be advised, also, that the two players involved are suspended pending investigation."

Boots' resembled an Arizona thermometer in July. The red climbed to his face. He was so flustered the words came out in spurts.

"You can't suspend me…Who the hell suspends Boots Anderson…You can take this college and stuff it. You can't fire me…I just quit."

So he did. So also did all the assistants. No one, they proclaimed in unison, would stick around a school that let a great coach like Boots go.

CHAPTER 8

Percival Pickens had sharp features. He had a pointed nose, protruding cheek bones but almost no chin. I instantly lacked confidence in him. He was too thin to be trusted. His eyes were squinty, and always looking elsewhere. That he did not look at me when he spoke could be forgiven, but not the fact that he never eyeballed the attractive Shirley Tate and her pretty blue eyes, her striking black hair, bronzed skin and long legs.

Search committees are a golden opportunity for patronage. Through selection of such groups, the school president can reward well-heeled alums for contributions, soothe angry faculty people and add to a democratic facade by picking students.

Time precluded such niceties. The president needed an immediate search committee to find an acceptable nominee quickly. It all came down at a meeting the day after Boots departed.

Who to pick?

Dr. White pointed to Pickens and said, "You." and pointed to me and said, "you, too, Bull."

You could see the wheels turning in his head. In the interest of being politically correct, he needed a woman. He nodded at Shirley, and said, "And you, too, Ms. Tate. You three will be our search committee. "

Dr. White later acknowledged in the public prints that he would have preferred a larger committee but pointed to the pressure of the time schedule. Boots was booted after the Sept.27 game. He was officially ousted on was Sept. 29. The search committee was formed on Sept. 30. Fortunately, the Rattlers had a bye on Oct. 4. But Dr. White insisted Southwestern must have a new coach in place by Oct. 6, at the latest. The team could not be expected to operate as it was, under student assistants.

Pickens convened our committee the next day. He made it clear he would be operating as a committee of one. "I'll be back to you in five days with a new coach."

Unsaid but understood was that ratification by the full committee would be automatic.

It was a blatant power play. But I was relieved, not disturbed. I realized, as Pickens apparently did not, that it would be impossible to hire a new, full-time head coach in mid season.

Pickens gave it a good try. He first called Joe Gibbs, recently retired as the Washington Redskin coach. Gibbs once had been an assistant at the University of Arizona and several times had expressed interest in returning to the state.

Gibbs was polite but kissed off Pickens with, "If I wanted to be a head coach again I'd do it in the NFL."

Undaunted, Pickens moved on to George Seifert, recently ousted as the San Francisco coach. Good choice. The gray-haired Seifert was intelligent, and an obvious gentleman.

"I have not tried to recruit a kid in since 1980 and I'm not sure I want to start again now," said Seifert. After being fired by the Arizona Cardinals, Gene Stallings had coached Alabama to the national championship and had retired to his ranch in Texas.

"I loved Arizona and the people there but I have had opportunities in both the NFL and large universities to return to coaching," he told Pickens "If I wouldn't go to one of the places for a full-time job, why would I come to a relatively unknown school like Southwestern?" Two other former NFL coaches were contacted. "You got to be kidding," said Sam Wyche.

"This is some kind of prank, right?" asked Jerry Glanville. "Who put you up to this, Lee Corso? "

A tad nervous by now, Pickens tried a new tack. He moved on to ex-coaches who were working regularly as on-the-air commentators.

This had been a fruitful spawning ground. It was a productive step taken by Mike Ditka and Dick Vermiel in the NFL as well as Pat Riley and Doug Collins in the NBA.

Terry Donahue, formerly a successful coach at UCLA, at one point had considered employment in Phoenix as a coach in the now defunct U.S. Football League.

"I would not consider any job in which the school is on NCAA proba-tion and barred from bowl games for a year, " Donahue told Pickens.

Actually, Southwestern had put itself on probation and imposed the bowl ban for one year. This is a common ploy of NCAA rules violators. Self-punishment lets the NCAA point to the fact the system is working. Another mitigating factor was the removal of the coaching staff and involved players. The NCAA ratified the school's action.

Lou Holtz, recently at Notre Dame, would not consider the post but did add, "However, I am available to speak at football banquets."

Mike Gottfried, ESPN commentator who had coached with success at Pittsburgh and Kansas, actively sought the Arizona State job in 1992.

"You think I'm crazy or something?" Gottfried asked Pickins. "Sure, I'd consider that job. But not now. Where in hell do you go out and find available assistants this time of year. And how do you put in your system at mid season. You better go out and beg one of Boots' assistants to stick around."

That, alas, had been tried earlier. Loyalty to Boots ran deep in these guys. No way would they consider replacing the railroaded head coach, they said.

Pickens had presumed the coaching search would lead him up the intercollegiate ladder, but it now seemed an anchor destined to drag him down.

Pickens called the president, who then called an emergency meeting of the search committee on Friday. Fine. Shirley and I would be glad to see the other third of the committee, who had been completely out of touch since Tuesday.

Percival couldn't get the words out: He had failed in his promised whirlwind search, but couldn't bring himself to admit it.

Instead, he said only that he had learned, as he had expected to learn, how difficult the search was. He listed the obstacles: Ex pros didn't want to recruit; No one wanted to take over at mid season; the uncertainty of probation and ineligible players plus the problem of lining up a staff.

At which point, Pickens, the singularly unsuccessful one-man search committee, returned the other two committee members to active status.

He turned to Shirley and said, "You, Ms. Tate, are responsible for our current problems. If you hadn't had that damned press conference, none of this would have happened. How do you propose to solve the problem?"

Shirley smiled, bringing a fist to her mouth to hide the beginnings of a laugh. She could recognize a buck being passed. She deserved no blame. She did not break rules. She only tried to enforce them.

Shirley turned to me and said, "Bull, if you hadn't talked me into the press conference, we wouldn't have had this problem. We might have computer fraud, cheating coaches and illegal players. But we wouldn't have had this problem. How do you propose to solve this problem?"

President White, privately amused, had experience getting committees back on track.

"Bull," he said, "No one holds you or Ms. Tate responsible but you, Bull, have been around athletics longer than the rest of us. Any ideas?"

"Well, sir, I think we have to face the fact that we can not at this time under these circumstances hire a full-time permanent coach worthy of the position. We could go out and find a high school coach somewhere who would jump ship. But that would be unfair to the high school and to our athletes. The solution is obvious. We have to hire an interim coach, and interim assistants to help him."

Pickens interrupted. "Well, sir, I once coached high school football."

It was a measure of our composure that no one snickered. I proceeded as if nothing had been said because, indeed, nothing of value had been.

"So where do we find interim coaches?" President White asked.

I shrugged, welcoming the chance to upstage Pickens in his quest of Brownie points.

"The Kelly girls don't stock temporary coaches. But because we are where we are, a great destination place for retirees, the area is overrun with old coaches.

"Just look around you, gentlemen. And lady. There are a bunch of possibilities. Guys like Dan Devine. He coached at Arizona State, Missouri, the Green Bay Packers and Notre Dame. There must be a couple of dozen other recent football coaches who have retired to the Valley.

"Coaches, in case you haven't noticed, have enlarged egos. Give these guys a chance to come back to coaching for a season and they'll jump at it. Just let me talk to Devine about it."

"But," said Pickens.

And that's as far as he got. President White interrupted, "Do it, Bull. Motion before the committee. All in favor, say aye. Motion passed unanimously."

One did not need to be particularly acute to note that athletic director Harrison Johnston had no spot on the search committee. It bugged Johnston, but no more than it bugged Justin White that Johnston had been so adamant concerning the security of the school's computer system and so defensive of Boots Anderson.

"I also am announcing another change in our athletic department," said White. "I am announcing today that I am relieving Harry Johnston as athletic director. His replacement as interim athletic director will be Bull Bullington. Any objections?"

"Hell, yes," I said. "In becoming sports information director, I already am straining Peter's Principle. If I am already beyond my level of competency as an SID, how could I expect to be competent as an AD?"

White shrugged and smiled. "Bull you have a lot to learn. This principle supersedes Peter's Principle: The higher one advances in athletic administration, the easier it is to fake it. And don't tell me an old sports columnist can't fake his way through it. I've seen you turn out columns in 10 minutes without having one new fact. Besides, it's just interim. You're my man, Bull."

CHAPTER 9

Shirley and I visited Devine, a coach I had covered at various spots during four decades. Taking Shirley was not the mistake I feared it might become. Devine personally held Ms. Tate guilty of sabotaging Southwestern's football program. He could forgive the press conference but not the fact that she refused to make academic concessions for athletes.

This was a strange stance for Devine, who had emphasized education along with athletics. He had a 93–37–1 record at Missouri. Impressive? Yes, but not as impressive as this: In his 13 years, 98 percent of his football players at Missouri graduated and 30 per cent got advanced degrees. His program was built on classy and intelligent athletes.

Shirley took a verbal paddling for not being more flexible with at-risk athletes, minor punishment which was quickly forgotten as she made her presentation. Well, it was not a presentation so much as an offer: Would you like to be interim coach at Southwestern for the rest of the year?

Devine's eyes widened. Of particular interest was the fact that he hesitated not a whit. Dan said firmly, "Yes."

Devine has an ego, which he attempts rather poorly to hide under a facade of humility. He doesn't need the buttering up as much as the attention which is lavished on the head coach. Craving for it is almost an addiction.

As a head coach, Devine relied on a student manager to serve as his personal hand maiden.

Devine is convinced he sweats more than most. He takes a lot of showers. A student manager stands by with three or four towels, which he requires to dry himself. That, he misses.

Another student manager had to be ready with a scarf which Dan wraps around his neck, even on 106-degree days. His neck, he will tell you, was injured in an auto accident. He misses the scarf-bearer too.

Devine's wife, Jo, an angel who fights a continuing battle with MS, shined his shoes when he was coaching. He claimed he did not have the time to do it himself.

He's not picky about food, but he is picky about the special service which nearly always goes with a head coaching job. He will order a cup of coffee, never touch it but insist it must be emptied before hot coffee is poured into it. And pity the maitre d who mispronounces his name.

Even after retiring from Notre Dame, Devine was flattered when Temple came after him. It was a chance to get back in the limelight. He gave it serious thought. When Missouri asked him to become interim athletic director, he quickly accepted. Hired for a year, he stayed for three and did much better than was expected in raising dough and uniting alumni factions.

So, it was not surprising that he leaped at the Southwestern interim job. It was suggested that he bring with him other coaches who had retired in the valley. Mentioned were Frank Kush and Al Onofrio, who had coached under Devine, and Chuck Fairbanks, who had played under him at Michigan State. He also was well acquainted with the other two suggested aides, Darryl Rogers and Jack Mitchell.

"That would be a hell of a staff," he said. "But all of them are head coaches. It would be awkward to ask any of them to go back to being assistants. What I think we should do is this: Let's make each of them head coach for one game. That way, they can look ahead—which, we, as card-carrying coaches, were not permitted to do when we were full time employees.

"Tell you what. The Onofrios were coming over for a cookout Sunday night anyway. I'll ask the other guys over, and we'll have a decision that night. Bull, why don't you and Shirley come, too. If we get them to agree, we should set up a team meeting early on Monday."

CHAPTER 10

I am glad I went to the cookout. It was a chance to see Devine recruit. His low-key recruiting, I suspect, was the key to his success. His was not the hard-sell approach of a tent evangelist. He was more like the kindly old uncle offering friendly advice.

Dan approaches problems through the side door. He talks in tangents, forever branching off into different subjects, although in the end he usually manages to tie them all together.

On this night of the cookout, Devine started on a tangent. He recalled a great play call by Mitchell in a Kansas-Missouri game. It was fourth and eight from the Missouri eight-yard line. A touchdown then would have assured Kansas the win.

"Remember what you called, Jack?" he asked.

Jack probed through his memory bank and came up blank.

"One of the greatest calls I ever saw," said Devine. "You call an inside screen pass to John Hadl. We got him, but it was just luck. In no way were we set up for that play. Hadl was playing halfback. It wasn't until the next year you moved him to quarterback. Right."

Jack nodded in agreement. Then, he recalled a "sucker shift" Devine had used against him. The shift was not designed to move personnel, but to move the opposition offsides. Kansas bit, and the five-yard penalty came at a crucial juncture.

I remember Devine being filled with righteous indignation when in the post-game interview I suggested he had used the sucker shift unethically to pull the foe offsides.

"That's an unfair and untrue accusation," he said, fixing me with an evil eye.

But here, 35 years later in the warmth of camaraderie, he did admit to Mitchell it was, indeed, a sucker shift designed only to get that needed five yards.

"But I wouldn't have done it if we hadn't needed it to win," Devine told Mitchell.

There, friends, is college coaching, in a nutshell.

It was that kind of night. Old memories were revived. Old friendships were renewed.

And old trick plays were reviewed. It was neat how Devine steered the conversation that way, first with the sucker shift, and then by asking Fairbanks to recite the best trick play ever pulled against him.

Chuck pondered that one and ducked a direct answer, but looked back to a memorable moment in the 1970 Bluebonnet Bowl, a 24–24 tie with Alabama.

"You always went in against Bear Bryant knowing he would pull one on you sometime, somewhere," Fairbanks said. "There are about eight minutes left. It's fourth and six for Alabama on the Oklahoma 25. We blitz. So we have man-to-man coverage in the secondary. We had every man covered but one. That's the quarterback. The quarterback hands off to the halfback, Johnny Musso.

"Musso goes right, pulls up and throws back across the field to the quarterback, Scott Hunter. He's the only guy we don't cover. It goes for a touchdown and gives them a 24–21 lead. We kick a field goal at the end to tie, but that pass back to the quarterback is the one I'd most like to have back."

The trick play was the swizzle stick that stirred the conversation.

The former Big Eight coaches recalled the "Bumarooskie," a fake kick popularized by Nebraska. This was a rather daring but largely successful play. The center faked his snap to the punter, and left the football laying on the ground. One of the big Nebraska guards picked up the ball, and waited until traffic passed him by. Then he doubled up to hide the football and proceeded untouched down the sideline.

Good one. They all agreed. "And how about the swinging gate?" said Onofrio.

This was first used in the Big Eight by Bud Wilkinson at Oklahoma. It usually is pulled out of the mothballs on field goals or extra points. The center rushes up over the ball with the place-kick holder and the kicker directly behind him. The other eight players are stationed off to the left of the center. It's no big deal if the defense adjusts. But seeing the center at the end of the line gives defenses problems. If too many defenders are set wide toward the obvious strength, a quick pitchout can be run in the other direction. Failure to adjust sets up a power play to the left.

Devine, ever the genial host, made a rather obvious move to involve Darryl Rogers. Darryl and Kush were the only ones without a Big Eight background.

"What was your favorite trick play, Darryl," he asked.

"This is back when I'm at Fresno State," said Rogers. Coaches favor the present tense in their story-telling mode for some reason. "We open against Cal Poly. We decide to run an onside kick on the first play. Everybody thought that was a gutsy call. And it was. But the damned kicker missed the ball. It was the best onside kick I've ever seen. It surprised everybody, including me."

The bull session was rolling. Every coach puts in a so-called gimmick play every week. Most gimmick plays rarely make their way off the practice field. They usually are installed only to relieve the monotony for players. Few coaches have the courage to use them. Coaches convince themselves each and every down is too important to waste on a trick play.

By now, the coaches were relaxed, delighting in reliving old times. They had circled the wagons around Devine, who was doing a good job of burning good meat on the charcoal broiler.

The stage was set. The audience was loose, doting on the good old days. A perfect set up, this, for Devine to make his pitch to the other coaches:

"Ever think what fun it would be to go back and run the trick plays you never used because you didn't have guts to do it?"

The coaches nodded in the affirmative. What the hell. Devine was supplying the beer.

"And did you ever think what fun it would be to coach if you could tell the alums or the press or some players' dad to stick it.

"And if you could tell a bitchy player, no matter how good he was, to shove off.

"And if you wouldn't have to recruit anybody, or put up with agents."

By now the coaches' eyes lit up. There were mumbles, then laughter and satisfied grins as they ran the interesting possibilities through their minds.

Onofrio then stood. I'll always feel Dan had set him up earlier to ask the question.

"Sounds great, Dan," Onofrio said. "But this is too good to be so. Where would you find this impossible job? Somewhere on the other side of St. Peter?"

Dan smiled, paused for suspense, and said, "Right here. Before your eyes. No moves. We all become the coaches at Southwestern for the rest of the year. They're in a bind. And we are the only logical answer. They already have come to me with this proposal. I think it's great. We get good money. And, we can do it our way.

"There's only one catch," Devine concluded. "We have to decide tonight. There's only a week to get ready for the next game, Saturday against Nebraska here."

Great opening game for a new staff, huh? But these guys had nothing to lose.

Onofrio and Mitchell had only to postpone their weekly golf games. Kush, who works at a boys ranch for wayward kids, was sure he could get a leave. Publicity for the boys camp would more than offset his absence. Fairbanks had only recently retired from a company which turned vacant property into high end golf courses.

Rogers faced the biggest problem, as athletic director at Southern Connecticut, but he was going to retire at year's end. He already had an assistant groomed to take his place.

So, it was virtually a done deal before the coaches left Divine's house. They left stuffed with steak and filled with eagerness. Most were surprised that the thought of returning to coaching could stir up such a fire in their guts.

CHAPTER 11

This sudden coaching change prompted a battle of the ages. Old vs. young. The young whippersnappers of the media knocked the idea of has-beens taking over a program that had gone to a bowl the previous year.

One talk show host, predictably, called the coaching committee "the over-the hill gang."

Oft-maligned elders, residing in the retirement areas ringing Phoenix, lit up talk show telephones with rebuttals.

"When you get over the hill, you pick up speed," said a somewhat shaky voice.

Said another senior, "These guys aren't over the hill. They're only on the back nine."

Senior citizens. quickly adopted the old coaching coots as their own. They had something to cheer. And they united with a surprising fervor to put down young critics of the Fossils.

And, there were critics. One talk-show caller suggested rocking chairs not benches on the sidelines. And another wondered if Geritol would be substituted for Gatorade. How about adding a trainer just for varicose veins, asked another.

Poison pen in hand, Bill "Scoop" Simon wrote in the state's leading newspaper, The Arizona Republic, the following:

"The resurrection of Dan The Devine and all these other has-beens raises questions concerning the sanity of the administration at Southwestern. What in hell are these Football Fossils doing there? Are they AARP rejects? Did they lose their Medicare or their minds?"

Football Fossils. The name stuck. It had a nice, alliterative ring and was adopted by unanimous consent by the coaching committee. It beat out Recycled Relics, Mouldy Mentors, Cranky Coaches, Grumpy Grandpas, Gridiron Golden Boys, Old Coaching Coots and other suggestions.

If the facts be known, the old coaches enjoyed being at the center of this controversy. Hell, it was just like the old days, when they developed thick skins. It was fun to hear the critics, particularly when it was OK to thumb collective noses at them.

Satisfying the public and the press was of little consequence to the Fossils. They hadn't been able to do that even as full-time coaches. So why sweat?

But it was important to gain the confidence of the players. Which is why the first official step was a team meeting on the same Monday the deal was firmed up with college brass.

This was no easy job. The squad was beset by suspicions and reservations. Overaged coaches, each taking over as head coach for only one week. Sounded strange, if not insane. Where did that leave young men who pictured Southwestern as their stepping stone to the NFL?

So it was a hostile audience the Fossils faced in their first team meeting. They came, the Rattlers players did, to meet the Football Fossils, who were to be the Southwestern coaches.

The audience was filled with sullen faces and angry voices. Questions were more a challenge than an inquiry. The scene resembled a mutiny about to happen. It was like inviting the NAACP to a Klan meeting.

These players felt they had been deserted, by presidential decree, Pres. White's decree that is. They had liked Boots Anderson. They liked his assistants. What they saw up on the stage were a bunch of silver-haired old fogies whose football days were long since over.

"Where did they find these guys," one player whispered to another, "in Jurassic Park?"

Replied the second player, "Put those guys in a race with a pregnant woman and they'd come in third."

Said another, "Bet they don't buy any green bananas."

These embittered players had gathered in the same steamy mini-auditorium where Shirley Tate's press conference had touched off the whole weird scenario.

I was elected to introduce the coaches. More at home with keyboards than microphones, I came with lines written out. I quoted first from Satchell Paige, the former great Negro baseball pitcher and philosopher.

"Age is mind over matter, Satch once told us. If you don't mind, it don't matter."

No smiles. No laughs. None of the audience had ever heard of Satchell.

I gulped and continued. "And it was also Satch who said, 'How old would you be if you didn't know how old you are.' "

More silence.

Ignoring the cool reception, I proceeded to introduce the new coaching staff—Devine, Kush, Onofrio, Fairbanks, Mitchell and Rogers and recited their coaching credentials. Players stifled yawns.

Perhaps to validate the fact that I was one of the boys, I wore short-short gym shorts. As I continued to talk, scattered snickers swept through the audience. I wasn't saying anything funny but each word brought more laughter.

Finally, Onofrio stepped forward and whispered in my ear. My eyes turned downward to the bottom of my short-short shorts.

Apparently, the jockey strap I was wearing had been washed too many times. At any rate, part of my private parts had dropped out and were dangling in full view of this amused audience.

Let it be admitted that I was not quick with the quip but my memory bank served me well in disasters. I was lucky at this particularly touchy moment to remember a similar incident at a coaching clinic. The speaker, Dr. Forrest E. "Phog" Allen, the basketball coaching great at Kansas, looked at his exposed vital parts and said then what I repeated at this time:

"Gentlemen, a dead bird never falls out of its nest."

It brought down the house. Laughter cascaded through the hostile audience. Smiles replaced frowns. What the heck, they figured, guys like that couldn't be all bad, even if they wore hairpieces and earpieces.

Devine, sensing the right moment, arose and opened the meeting to questions. The questions or concerns could be addressed to any or all of the coaches on the platform, he announced.

An enormous guy on the front row stood. His shadow eclipsed two more rows. He spoke softly with the high voice of a choirboy. The voice and his physique didn't match.

"My name is Michael Matuszak. I'm an offensive lineman. I'm hopeful of making it in the pros. And I want to know if you can give me the training I need. I am 6 foot 10, and weigh 310 pounds. What are you going to do with me?"

"Put you in a uniform that fits," said Devine.

"Then we'll turn you over to Frank Kush. Although too small, Frank was a starting guard at Michigan State and he turned out great offensive linemen as an assistant and as a head coach.

"But you'll have to work to play for him. It won't be like those oversized hunks you see too often in the NFL now. You can't make it with us if you stand up and just rooster fight with the defender. We want linemen who move people out, who make holes, and not those guys who feel like they've done a good job if they make the other guy run around them."

If the Rattlers had a leader it had to be Bobby Joe Jackson. He was born to quarterback. His dad was a Texas high school coach who coached Bobby Joe from the cradle on. Bobby Joe was a handsome, well mannered, a yes-sir. no-sir kind of a guy.

"We are very honored to have men of your stature as coaches," said Bobby Joe. "And I hope you won't misunderstand this but all my life has been aimed at becoming an NFL quarterback. Boots was the perfect coach for that. Pardon me for saying this, but I feel like my career has been knocked for a loop."

Devine replied, "Hey, I've always been a passing coach. When I was at Missouri we threw seven interceptions against Penn State in the Orange Bowl. Don't tell me we were afraid to pass.

"I had Bart Starr and John Hadl at Green Bay. It's true both were at the end of their careers. But I also had Joe Montana at Notre Dame when he was just starting.

"Darryl Rogers is a great passing coach. He was coaching the West Coast offense before it had a name. He had Mike Pagel, who went into the NFL. Pagel was recruited by Kush. But, hell, Kush recruited a lot of them. . Kush has sent at least a dozen quarterbacks to the NFL. "

One small group off the left started to chuckle. It was obvious they were amused by the question which was rehearsed on them, to wit: "Do old guys become impotent?"

Jack Mitchell, in his early 70s, answered this one. "Dunno know, sonny. Call me back in a few years."

Linebacker Joe Fridena was the team smartass. An assistant coach once said there was not enough mustard in the concession stands to cover this hot dog. Fridena stood up on the back row and said loudly enough to be heard by all:

"Why should we put up with a tough guy like Kush. Like if I wanted this I would have stayed in reform school. Time's passed you guys by. Today's players don't have to put up with that ass-kicking, helmet-rattling stuff. How do you learn anything that way?"

Kush is not as big as his reputation. He played as a 5–10 190-pound offensive guard at Michigan State. He remains at his playing size, still stout and tightly packed. But he oozes an intensity which makes him grow right before your eyes.

Daggers danced in Kush's eyes as he grabbed the microphone. But before he could get a word out, the mike was yanked from his hands by a taller, younger man.

This was the first big surprise of several to come. Danny White was a Hall of Fame quarterback at Arizona State, and played for 13 years (eight as a starter) with the Dallas Cowboys.

White smiled down on Kush, his old coach, and said, " Let me handle this one, coach. My name is Danny White."

No introduction was necessary. Even those new to the area knew about his exploits as a player and his growing reputation as the coach of the

Phoenix arena club, which had won two championships. "So, you're afraid of not learning under Coach Kush. Let me tell you this, young man: If you listen to Coach Kush, and do what he tells you, he will make you as good as you can be. Yeah, he's tough. I had some apprehensions going into the NFL. But I had confidence I could handle anything they could dish out because he had made us mentally tough. He had a real strengthening affect on all the players."

White, it developed, was the first of several former players to infiltrate the meeting. That they showed up on one day's notice was a tribute to the Fossils and to White. White, upon hearing about the first squad meeting, called other players.

Next, to take the podium without introduction was Johnny Roland, an All-American at Missouri as an offensive halfback and a defensive corner-back. They don't make 'em like that now.

Roland, a super prep out of Corpus Christi, Texas, had first signed a letter of intent with Oklahoma. But the letter was not binding in those days. Missouri lured him away from the Sooners.

So highly regarded was Roland that Oklahoma sent an assistant coach into the Missouri athletic dining hall trying to lure him out. Roland was an outstanding running back with the St. Louis Cardinals, a team he now serves as an assistant.

"Coach Devine wasn't a real strong x and o kind of a guy," said Roland. "He let his assistants coach. He was more of a organizational, motivational kind of a guy."

"But wasn't he almost too low key?" asked a player.

"Not on the sideline," replied Roland. "It was well documented and well chronicled that he could throw the clipboard as far as anyone in the league. It didn't take much. If things weren't going right, there would go the clipboard."

Roland was primarily a defensive back under defensive coordinator Onofrio, although he carried the ball in tight situations in key games.

"And Coach Onofrio," Roland continued. "Well, you'll never be around a smarter defensive coach."

A player, who wisely chose to remain anonymous, spoke from a seated position in the middle of the audience.

"Who the hell is this Mitchell guy? And what's he doing coaching."

"Well," Mitchell told the youngster. "I had to coach. I was too nervous to steal and too dumb to lie."

Questioning Jack's credentials was understandable, considering the age group asking the questions. Mitchell, first of Oklahoma's great option quarterbacks, was head coach at Wichita State, Arkansas and Kansas, but had not coached since 1966.

Mitchell could have talked his way out of the touchy situation. He was a master of BS. But he did not get a chance. The mike was yanked from his hands by John Hadl, who is equally full of BS. Hadl had played for Mitchell at Kansas and had an illustrious career with the San Diego Chargers.

"So, you want to know who Mitchell is, huh?" said Hadl. "Without question, he's the greatest recruiter of all time and the most enthusiastic coach I've ever been around. But Jack also has the ability to hire great staff people and to win.

"Is that enough? Nope. I want you to know how lucky you are. Mitchell is a unique guy with a great personality and he's smarter than hell. He got rich after he left Kansas. He bought a newspaper in Wellington, Kan., then added a TV cable network. He got in with an oil field equipment group. There were in on 11 straight oil wells that hit. Here's something not many know. Kansas fired him but he recently donated $50,000 to the new Kansas athletic building."

Another kid stood up in the audience and asked, "If he's such a great recruiter who did he recruit?

"He recruited me. He also recruited Gale Sayers. Ever hear of him?"

I don't know about today's kids but people of my era were well acquainted with Sayers. He was making those Barry Sanders' type moves before there was a Barry Sanders.

Sayers is best remembered as a Chicago Bear running back. But my memories of him go back to a college game at Oklahoma State in 1962 when Gale set a Big Eight single game rushing record after being kicked out for fighting.

He didn't understand he had been banished. Neither did Mitchell. Or, so they said. Sayers reentered the game a few plays later, and ran for the needed 10 yards to push his rushing total to a record 283 yards. At that point the official recognized Sayers and booted him again.

By now, the audience was a-buzz. This was big-deal stuff.

The following question was addressed to Rogers: "I'm looking to play baseball, sir, as well as football. And we've got a track guy on our squad. Will that cause any problems?".

"No," said Rogers. "By the time you get around to those other sports we'll be out of here."

But that was all he got to say because Mike Pagel, one of his old quarterbacks who had played for three different NFL teams, nudged him away from the microphone with an affectionate bear hug.

"This one's right down my alley," Pagel said. "Let me tell you about me. I always played baseball and football for Darryl. No questions asked. I can remember going from spring football practice over to the baseball diamond carrying my shoulder pads.

"You want more? Let me tell you about Kirk Gibson, who became a all-time baseball great. Kirk is a big guy (6–3, 227) playing as a wide receiver for Darryl at Michigan State. One day, the baseball coach comes over to Darryl and tells him that Kirk has baseball talents, according to some of his players. Darryl goes and talks to Gibson, tells him it's all right and suggests he go play baseball. And he did, in college, in the pros. It's all in Gibson's book.

"Darryl also had an Olympic sprinter in Ron Brown. And a lot of people forget that Reggie Jackson came to Arizona State under Kush on a football scholarship."

White returned to the podium and apologized that two other players he invited couldn't make it. They were Steve Owens, a Heisman Trophy winner under Fairbanks at Oklahoma, and Montana, a star under Devine at Notre Dame.

White said, however, that he, Hadl, Roland and Pagel would stick around to talk to interested Rattlers. And so, the meeting none of the Rattlers wanted to attend went on for four hours.

The testimonials left the players surprised and impressed with the Fossils. But no more surprised, probably, than the schedule posted on the bulletin board outside the meeting room. This schedule was a walk into the park compared to that faced by most college teams.

Football Practice Schedule

Sunday: Players off except for those who need training room attention.

Monday: Players off except for one hour review of game film at 4 p.m.

Tuesday: Practice 3 to 5 p.m. Put in offense.

Wednesday: Practice 3 to 5 p.m. Put in defense.

Thursday: Practice 3 to 5 p.m. Special teams, and touch up on offense and defense.

Friday: Travel. If at home, one hour walkthru at 3 p.m.

Saturday: Game. Guarantee: No night workouts. No workout exceeding two hours.

Academics

Tutoring: Four new tutors added. Available at your request if appointment made two days in advance. New optional courses offered at 2 p.m. on Sundays called Pro Football 101. Will stress basics needed to coach or to play pro football. Will have experts in media relations and in labor negotiations. Special private consultations available on how to pick agents and financial advisors. This is no-credit course but we hope to convince university to offer it for credit in future.

GAME SCHEDULE

(Head coach for game listed in parentheses)

Date	Where	Game	Head Coach
Aug.30	Home	SW 13, Oregon State 7	
Sept.6	Home	SW 17, TCU 7	
Sept.13	Away	SW 10, Indiana 7	
Sept.20	Away	SW 24, Temple 7	
Sept.27	Home	New Mexico State 27, SW 7	
Oct.4	bye		
Oct.11	Home	Nebraska at SW	Onofrio
Oct.18	Home	Mississippi at SW	Mitchell
Oct.25	bye		
Nov.1	Away	SW at Texas	Fairbanks
Nov.7	Home	Arizona at SW	Kush
Nov.14	Away	SW at Michigan	Devine
Nov.21	Away	SW at Washington State	Rogers

CHAPTER 12

There is no place like Nebraska Dear old Nebraska U. Where the girls are the fairest, the boys are the squarest Of any old place that you knew.

Sweet tune, this, for Cornhusker football fans. But not so sweet for opponents. The fight song is played with exuberance by the red-clad Nebraska band each time the Huskers score, which is often.

When repeated often, the marching song takes on all the sweetness of a dirge, scarring eardrums and wounding psyches of falling foes. Under its frustrating spell, opposing coaches take unusual and desperate measures.

Consider Dan Devine. Constant reruns of the dirge turned his stomach when his Missouri team lost 35–0 at Nebraska in 1966. During the off season, Devine dispatched an aide to Lincoln, Neb., to pick up a record of the fight song.

On the week of the 1967 game with Nebraska, the Missouri locker room reverberated with that Husker marching song. It was played non-stop at the loudest level the amplifier could attain.

"There is no place like Nebraska, dear old Nebraska U."

Over and over. Louder and louder. Grating at nerve ends.

So the stage was set for Devine's Friday afternoon pep talk. The team gathered in the locker room. The Husker fight song blared over the loudspeakers. Shouting over the din, Devine demanded that an assistant remove the offending record and bring it to him.

This was to be Devine's big scene. He snatched the record out of the aide's hands and announced, "I'm tired of this damned record. I'm going to get rid of it forever."

With that, he slammed the record on a table. It did not break. Then the coach grasped the record on two edges and banged it over his knee. Not a crack appeared.

And they say records are made to be broken.

Devine then tried breaking the record by throwing it at the concrete floor. No luck. So Devine jumped up and down on the record.

It would not break. Titters filled the locker room. Players covered their faces, to hide smiles. Even faithful aide Al Onofrio could not choke back a laugh.

Finally, in a desperate face-saving move, Devine sailed the record out a window, and said with some relief, "Now we're rid of that danged thing forever."

So everything went wrong in the Friday pep talk, but on the following day every thing went right as Missouri won 10–7.

Onofrio told the story to the Southwestern players before their first practice under him.

"The moral of the story," he said, "is that games are won not by pep talks but by players trying hard and coaches planning well."

The public has been brainwashed to believe upsets spring from eloquent speeches by emotional coaches. Maybe they saw Knute Rockne's Gipper speech in the movie or heard tapes of Vince Lombardi browbeating his Green Bay Packers.

That, be it submitted, is not the stuff from which upsets necessarily are made. Take Onofrio. He is a laid back, soft spoken and rarely excitable coach—the antithesis of a Rockne or Lombardi. But Onofrio is a giant killer of the first order. His seven Missouri teams were mediocre (38–41–0) but had a knack of rising to surprising heights against the best teams. Biggest of his big upsets were over Notre Dame, Alabama, Southern Cal and Ohio State.

That made Onofrio an ideal choice to coach the Rattlers' first game under the Fossils. Onofrio was not snowed by the Nebraska reputation. As the defensive coordinator at Missouri, he drove the Huskers nuts with his trademark defense, the seven diamond, that is seven men on the line of scrimmage, one middle linebacker and three deep defensive backs.

In his years as a Missouri defensive coordinator, the Tigers were 8–5 against the Huskers. As head coach, he was 3–4 against NU with vastly inferior teams. No other Big Eight coach of that era did better.

Even Onofrio's most disastrous loss to the Huskers, 62–0 in 1972, had a silver lining. The next week, Missouri beat heavily favored Notre Dame, 30–26.

That Notre Dame game provided the pattern for the Rattlers' preparations for the upcoming game with Nebraska. Getting ready to face the Fighting Irish, Onofrio started by throwing the film of the 62–0 loss to Nebraska into the waste can. And now, Onofrio started by trashing the film of the Rattlers' 28–10 loss to New Mexico.

"No point in looking at those films," Onofrio told his relieved players. "You know and I know you can play better than that."

The offense was pared down, polished. Onofrio added just one new wrinkle for the Huskers. Actually it was an old wrinkle revised. At the Devine cookout where the coaches had been recruited, the conversation settled into reruns of old trick plays.

The trick play resurrected for Nebraska was a combination of two gimmicks. At the cookout, Darryl Rogers told about the onside kick he once used at the start of a game. Great play, poor execution. The kicker whiffed the the football.

Onofrio then recalled a successful onside kick Kansas State used against Missouri in 1969. It was a weird contest, eventually won by Missouri, 41–38, but only after Kansas State moved fans to the edge of seats with two touchdowns within one minute late in the game. A 55-yard scoring pass by Lynn Dickey was followed by an onside kick, which set up another touchdown. It was this unusual onside kick that Southwestern was to resurrect against Nebraska.

On that muddy, rainy day in 1969, the K-State kicker interrupted his runup on the ball. He paused, looked down and said, "Damn it, I've got mud on my cleats."

While the K-State kicker kneeled to scrape his shoes, another K-Stater kicked off, dribbling the ball the required 10 yards. A teammate recovered.

History was to repeat. Like the Kansas State kicker of yesteryear, the Rattler kicker, Joe Don Hentzen, stopped his run toward the teed up football, and said, "Sorry, guys, I've got mud on my shoe."

He bent down on one knee to scrape the muddy shoe. The Huskers went into a parade rest. So transfixed were they that not one player stopped to think the field was not muddy—not in dry Arizona where the rainfall is less than 10 inches a year.

As Hentzen bent over his clean cleats, up stepped the guy next to him, ostensibly to offer condolences or help. Instead, he kicked the ball. It squirted through the front five Nebraskans, who were caught flat-footed. The officials, alerted to the play, grinned on the sly.

The kicker, Rod Norman, recovered on the 50-yard line. For the kicking team to get possession, the onside kick must travel at least 10 yards or be touched by the receiving team. Then it's up for grabs. Possession goes to the team recovering the kicked football.

Norman was playing in the first football game he had ever seen. But he had been thoroughly coached to pounce on his own kick after it had bounded the required 10 yards.

Norman was a sort of emergency sub. In the changeover of staffs, the Rattlers lost 16 players—two from cyberspace cheating and 14 who were disenchanted. It left Southwestern short of bodies to run the opposition's plays in practice. The Rattlers advertised for help in the student newspaper and on the campus radio station. To everyone's surprise, 14 volunteers showed up by Wednesday. Most were student-students, as opposed to what the NCAA presumptuously calls student-athletes. They were used primarily to hold dummies in blocking practice. But among these volunteers were four who would make an impact.

The four were actually athletes, although not football athletes. There were two from the basketball team—point guard Jose Garcia and power forward Muhammad Jones. Both had used up basketball eligibility but were in school finishing degrees. Then there was Ronald Owens, a world-class sprinter from the track team. He had never played football but an agent convinced him it might be more profitable to catch passes than other runners. Then there was Norman, a big rawboned kid who had come over from Australia to play tennis. He didn't make the tennis team, but hoped kicking skills learned in soccer and Australian football might get him a scholarship.

And they did. Norman's sweetly toed onside kick, and the recovery of same, resulted in a grant being awarded to him the following Monday.

One play does not a football game win. At least not on the game-opening play. But Norman's onside kick had an inordinately strong impact on the Huskers.

The Huskers had come to the contest worried about a supposedly haunted field, Kush field, on which they had lost four of their five Fiesta Bowl games.

And Coach Tom Osborne injected another negative by dwelling on Arizona's hot weather. Wary of heat, Osborne had his players work out indoors all week, with the thermostat turned up to 90 degrees. Hot stuff, huh?

Nebraska was unbeaten, ranked No. 5 in the country. But the successful kicking gamble stirred memory of the haunted house theory and left Huskers wondering about the heat, although the temperature was in the mid 80s.

Starting at midfield after recovering the opening kick, the Rattlers' fullback, Bill Bovine, slashed right for two yards. Tailback Tim Pruitt picked up six on a counter and quarterback Bobby Joe Jackson got a yard on a draw. Fourth and one at the Nebraska 41.

What to do? Hell, go for it. This was a staff immune to critics. The crowd erupted in approval as the Rattlers lined up to run for the one yard.

The Rattlers bunched up in a tight formation. Only one end was split. No. 81, he was. Announcers scrambled for a program. No. 81 was Ronald Owens. "A new guy," one fan whispered to another.

"Just a decoy," said another.

"I hear he's a sprinter," said the first fan. "Second place in the NCAA 100 meters last year."

To which his friend said, "But hell, this ain't no track meet. They won't throw to him."

In its goal line defense, Nebraska jammed the foe's tight end to prevent him from getting in a pass catching position. Owens drew only token traffic—one cornerback. And the cornerback was edging toward the middle when the ball was snapped.

Jackson faked to Bovine, put the ball on his hip and rolled right. There in the distant endzone he could see Owens, as lonely as a Maytag repairman. Jackson lofted the football in a soft catchable arc. Owens circled in a holding pattern beneath the descending ball. He pulled it to his bosom and, with a sick feeling, saw it bounce out. But it bounced back into his eager hands. A 41-yard touchdown pass.

Owens, so inspired by his first touchdown, did a celebration dance. It was a finger pointing, leg slapping routine—a sort of combination of the Texas Two Step and the Charleston.

Hentzen converted. Southwestern led 7–0 two minutes into the game.

Onofrio greeted Owens as he returned to the sideline with the perfunctory pat on the back but he then fixed the youngster with a stare and spoke in a voice loud enough to reach other players.

"Young man, I want you to know the coaching staff did not appreciate that endzone dance you did. As Vince Lombardi once told one of his Green Bay players in a similar situation, 'We want our players, upon reaching the endzone, to act like they've been there before.'"

Spectators showing up a couple of minutes late for the game and leaving a couple of minutes early would have missed all the scoring. Dull? Perhaps, but not to aficionados of defense.

Although badly outmanned, Southwestern walked a veritable tight rope. Among Nebraska's three turnovers were two fumbles and an interception—all three inside the Southwestern 20-yard line. That helped but so too did that seven-diamond defense, which was Onofrio's calling card.

It's a daring defense. It dares a foe to take to the air. Big and tall defensive ends are a key. Well that, and a middle linebacker versatile enough to stop the rush and drop back 15 yards in pass defense.

The seven diamond defense (7–1–3) is not complicated but Onofrio could not be expected to install it in three days. But Al was fortunate in that Boots Anderson's teams used a 7–1–3 goalline defense.

Some adjustments were made. A strong safety, Gus Franchoni, was moved into the middle linebacker spot. He was a savvy player, son of a high school coach. He was big enough to stop the rush, but not quite fast enough to cover passes. His know-how made up for deficiencies. The rangiest, fastest two outside linebackers, Simon Young and Maury Oliver, were turned into defensive ends. A few stunts were set up with the middle four defenders.

But, still, it was a crapshoot. The Rattlers gambled that their three deep defenders could cover wide receivers man-on-man. A dangerous gamble unless the quarterback could be kept off balance by a devastating pass rush.

That was the crack finally exploited by Nebraska with 58 seconds left. Osborne kept 10 of his 11 players in to protect the left-handed quarterback, John Farrington and sent one receiver, Rodger Johns, on a streak down the sidelines. The pass was completed for 45 yards to the one-yard line. The fullback bulled in from there, with 22 seconds left. Score: Southwestern 7, Nebraska 6.

Onofrio called time out and waved his defense over to the sideline for a conference.

"Trust me, men," said Onofrio, "I don't care how they line up, they are going for two points. If they are in a place kick formation, I want nine guys up front coming hard. Go for the holder. No angling for a blocked kick. No jumping to knock a kick down. The holder is a second-string quarterback capable of running or passing. I want him smothered before he can stand up. Do that and you win the game no one thought you could win."

And so it was that the quarterback-holder was bowled over like a helpless tenpin as he tried to stand up to pass.

Reporters surrounded Onofrio in the post game dressing room. Electronic people stuffed microphones down his throat.

One wanted to know about that fourth-and-one gamble that produced the only Southwestern score. Had he ever gambled like that. Had he ever had a more productive pass?

"Yes, as a matter of fact I have," Al said. "We were playing Nebraska in 1976. Our punter was having a bad day. We decided not to have him punt. But there we were on our own two-yard line, third and 10. The defense crammed in, convinced we wouldn't risk a pass so deep in our own territory. But our quarterback…he was Pete Woods…he throws a pass to Joe Stewart that goes for 98 yards and a touchdown."

Players had told reporters how Onofrio correctly predicted the fake kick for the two points. How, asked the reporters, could he read Osborne's mind.

"That's how Tom Osborne is," Onofrio said. "We beat him back in 1973 by 13–12 when he went for two and didn't make it.

"And then there was that Orange Bowl (1984) when he gave up a tie which would have won the national championship to go for two and a win against Miami. He's told me that he has never received so many letters supporting anything he ever did as that gamble he lost. Miami won (31–30)."

There you are. Onofrio has been there. Experience, the kind that comes with age, had been helpful to Onofrio and was to be helpful to the other Football Fossils.

CHAPTER 13

On the night of the Nebraska victory, and in the flush of triumph, Shirley Tate asked me to take her to the coaches' post-game drink. My knees turned weak. So did my voice. I gulped out a answer which in no way reflected my excitement over her invitation.

"Sure," I said.

It was a pleasant evening, perfect for beers and barbecue in Al Onofrio's backyard. My duty as an escort, I had presumed, was to fill in the conversational voids when the coaches and their wives spoke football. I was surprised. Shirley didn't need a translator. Her questions were pertinent, her understanding of the strategy obvious.

I had forgotten that New Mexico State game, where she had passed a critical test first against that loud bully in the stands and then that other loud bully with a laptop computer, Scoop Simon.

The party broke up about midnight. It was a night I wanted never to end, but it did end abruptly after I pulled up to the curb in front of Shirley's high-rise apartment building.

"I can find my way upstairs," she said as she opened the car door. "Great night, Bull. I appreciate it."

"Me too," I stammered. And without previous thought announced my birthday was Sept. 30, the following Wednesday, which it really wasn't.

"I usually go out for a nice dinner. Would you care to join me, say about 7 O'clock?"

"I'd be honored," she said. "I'll meet you in the lobby."

I had always been a Chevvy or Ford kind of guy. But I never had been an athletic director before. The new position deserved a new car.

On Tuesday, I shopped for a new car. It's an impossible search for the elusive bottom line. New cars need yet another accessory, a polygraph to weigh conflicting statements of the salesmen, the figure-crunchers, the used car appraisers and the closers.

Out of frustration, I relied on my heart. I fell in love with a golden Lincoln Continental, which came with a moon roof and a CD player. The salesman explained it was an executive car, driven only 4,000 miles by the owner's wife. In a confidential whisper from behind the back of his hand, he said he could get it for $32,000. I whipped out my checkbook.

Washed and shined, both car and owner showed up at 6:59 in the apartment parking lot. To impress my date, I had bought a CD of Mozart's piano concertos Nos. 23 & 27. The classics, I had learned, impress ladies more than John Phillip Sousa.

Neither the roll-back roof nor the fancy audio system impressed Shirley as much as the remote control which operated doors, trunk and alarm signal from a doo-dad on the key chain.

And I was impressed—as never before—by Shirley Tate. She wore a simple black dress that hugged her slim figure down to the ankles. She had found a pair of flats to wear instead of spiked heel shoes. As I correctly assumed, she wore the flats so we could be on a reasonably level playing field.

A single strand of pearls encircled her neck. For my viewing pleasure, she revealed a tiny touch of cleavage below the jewelry.

Proudly, I explained my new car. I showed her the remote but instead opened the passenger side with an old-fashioned key. Didn't want to show off too much.

Helpfully, Shirley reached over and pulled up the button unlocking the driver's side door. I slid in across the leather seats, inserted the key and turned it to the far right, the starter position. Nothing happened. No whir. No clicking. No nothing. Only a red face.

I opened the hood, which is what men always do in an emergency. There was a motor in there.

Reassured, I nodded, slammed the hood and returned to the fruitless key turning.

Shirley was a good scout, as they say. She avoided a snicker, but down deep, seemed to enjoy the amusing moment. But she was helpful. She stashed the pearls in her purse, figuratively rolled back the sleeves she did not have and helped. We pushed the car onto the driveway, hoping the slight incline might start the motor. No luck. A friendly motorist volunteered to jump start this silent monster. Nothing. Not even that click, click, click.

By now we were sweating, swearing and stained. I fought back tears. Perspiration dampened Shirley's black hair. A tiny rivulet of sweat rolled down into the cleavage. I was miserable.

And Shirley? At a later date she confided she had been amused, even had to fight back laughter. The specter of a proud new owner unable to start his expensive new toy, in looking back, was amusing.

As we stepped into emergency transportation, her Honda Accord, she had to stick in a needle.

"Happy birthday to you, happy birthday to you," she sang.

"Take that song and stuff if," I said in mock anger.

The Honda, wouldn't you know it, belched to life with the first turn of the key and delivered us without further problems to the circle drive in front of the Mansion Club.

The parking valet looked at the Accord and its disheveled passengers and asked in a snooty voice, "Did you have a reservation, sir?"

We did, although we were 45 minutes late. Shirley and I made quick repairs in rest rooms and were given a once over by the maitre 'd, who happened to be an old friend.

"Hey, Bull, you want one of those blazers we save for coatless guests."

"You know what you can do with that coat," I retorted sweetly.

After soaking up our first drink and first marvelous 360-degree view of the city, we were feeling normal.

The Mansion Club is the old Wrigley mansion. Yes, the chewing gum, Chicago Cub family. It's atop a peak just above the historic Biltmore hotel. Its classic rooms are decorated by Wrigley mementos. And its views. . well, they are unequaled in this desert Mecca. I opted for the sun room, a glass enclosed west porch from which the desert sunsets are incomparable.

Chef Robert Bland selected our menu and cooked it. I don't know what it was. Something French sounding. But it was great. A disastrous evening was rescued.

The Accord returned us to my marooned Continental. I wanted to give it one more chance before I took a cab home. The driver's door opened on command from the remote. I inserted the key, turned it and the engine purred smoothly.

"You better drive it home while you can, Bull," said Shirley.

I had looked forward to escorting my date to her door. But she was right. No point in tempting fate.

It was about 3 a.m. when I awoke in a cold sweat. Something I had seen in scanning the operating manual of the Continental returned to my mind. I ran to the garage and dug the manual out of the glove compartment.

Sure enough, there it was, listed under setting the alarm section. The security system included disabling the starter and was automatically set when the driver left the car and looked all the doors. To disarm the security and make the starter operative, one had to enter from the driver's side with key or remote.

Nothing to it. But remember, Shirley had flipped the door button open for me from inside the car. That didn't unlock the starter. So I tried several times the prescribed method of entering from the driver's side with key or remote. Damned if the starter did not work every time.

Dawn was only an hour or so away but I called Shirley and explained what happened. We both laughed about it. I like to think a bond had formed that night.

"Good night birthday boy," she cooed.

"Birthday? Oh. Yeah. Thanks. I do feel a little older."

CHAPTER 14

The problem, after a victory as huge as the upset of Nebraska, is to return to earth for the next game.

One coach wanted to sell the upcoming game with Mississippi as a frying pan-to-fire situation. Lurking thoughts of impending disaster was a time-honored coaching ploy. But the consensus of the staff was that players were too sophisticated to buy that hackneyed approach. Mississippi was 5–1, but clearly inferior to Nebraska.

It was, then, a happy coincidence—one of many that was to benefit the Fossils—that the Fossils' coach of the week was one who had deep-rooted, strong feelings about Mississippi. Coach Jack Mitchell transmitted his feelings to the players. His natural exuberance and penchant for exaggeration combined to get Rattler minds off Nebraska and on Mississippi.

In Mitchell's three-year stay at Arkansas, his biggest obstacle was the annual game with Mississippi. It was the money game. Mississippi and Arkansas are separated by the Mississippi River, on the banks of which were located the biggest plantations and richest people in both states.

Mitchell, first of a series of great Oklahoma option quarterbacks, features himself as a kicking-game specialist. He is the last of the quick-kick advocates. As a player, he set NCAA kick return records—largely because of the returns on which he reversed or faked reverses with Darrell Royal, later a coaching great at Texas.

Mitchell also is something of a con man. Oklahoma's 1947 Missouri game was a pivotal one. And at a pivotal point in the game, with Oklahoma nursing a 14–12 lead, Mitchell called time-out. He announced halfback George Brewer was going to carry the football and then pleaded with Brewer to pick up the needed two yards, and most of all, not fumble.

"So, boy I hit through there," Brewer recalls. "I must have had four guys on me. I went eight or nine yards, running as hard as I could. I go down, start reaching around. I don't have the ball. I thought, oh crap, I've fumbled. I'm almost in tears. Then I look up. There's Jack. He has the football. He's run 39 yards. He's going out on the one-yard line.

"He went through all that stuff just to get a decent fake out of me."

To Mitchell, no pains were too great to gain a slight edge. At Kansas, Mitchell called in a psychiatrist from the famous Menninger Clinic to hypnotize a tailback prone to fumbling into not fumbling. The kid was not hypnotized by the coin swinging to and fro, to and fro. But one of Mitchell's assistants, Don Fambrough, was. He toppled out of his chair.

Mitchell, ever a detail guy in the kicking game, rehearsed punters on how to react if the center snap sailed over their head. Practice paid in Arkansas' 1957 game with Mississippi at Memphis.

Shortly before halftime, a substitute snapper soared a snap far over the head of the punter. The punter retreated, recovered the ball and was able to get off an end over end, sidesaddle kick on the run.

To reach dressing rooms at halftime, both teams exited through the same tunnel. Mississippi's great coach, Johnny Vaught, was talking about the on-the-run punt with an aide. "I suppose that damn Mitchell's going to say he practices that," Vaught said.

Mitchell was within earshot. He nudged Vaught and said, "As a matter of fact we do."

At Arkansas, Mitchell was 2–1 against the highly-respected Vaught. Which was why the Fossils agreed to give him Southwestern's game against Ole Miss at Oxford, Miss.

Mitchell came up with a new kicking wrinkle for this one, the run-kick option featuring the school's refugee from Australian football, Rod Norman. Actually the run-kick option was not new but borrowed— which is true of most so-called innovations in football.

In 1990, Arizona State had another Australian football kicker, Brad Williams. Larry Marmie then was the head coach at ASU and now is an aide with the Arizona Cardinals. He called Mitchell to share his experience with Aussie kickers. The best play with an Aussie-trained kicker, he said, was the run-kick option. Williams would take off right. If the secondary came up, he booted an end-over-end kick on the run. If the secondary played back, Williams ran.

Rod Norman, Southwestern's Australian, had demonstrated his potential with the carefully-toed onside kick at Nebraska. On longer kicks, he had uncanny accuracy. The kicks, often bouncing 50 yards or more, could be aimed away from dangerous returners or out of bounds inside the 10-yard line.

Norman's kicking talents were ideally suited to the run-kick option. Norman kicked on the run naturally. He had been training for such things since he was a toddler. It is an intregal part of Australian football. Plus, Norman was big enough to run over people.

Mitchell and Norman, a free-spirited beer-drinking Aussie, hit it off right away. Mitchell never became accustomed to being called "mate" in every other sentence but gave Norman great leeway. On punt plays, either quick kicks or from deep punt formation, the savvy Aussie had a green light to run anytime he felt sure of making a first down.

Seldom has kicking been more important than it was that night in Oxford, Miss. A tropical storm touched off three days of rain. The field was drenched, suitable only for testing arks. Mud cleats didn't come long enough to provide footing. At game time, the rain was still falling—sideways, in sheets. The coaches met at midfield and talked about postponing. Officials intervened. The game was on regional television. Postponement was not an option.

The Ole Miss kicker slipped on the opening kickoff. The near-whiff traveled only 25 yards. The Rattlers started on their own 40-yard line with a play that astounded everyone.

Norman took a pitchout and sprinted to his right. The cornerback and safety started up and were stunned when Norman kicked on the run. The ball surfed crazily along the drenched turf. The Rattlers killed the ball on the Ole Miss 10.

Mississippi was cautious, running three times for a total of four yards, before punting. The Rattlers, having taken over on the 50, did the unbelievable. They option-kicked again on first down. The football rolled dead on the eight-yard line.

The Rattlers punted on first down on their first three possessions. On the fourth occasion, Norman took the pitchout, looked at the defense retreating, conditioned as it was to the first-down punts.

Norman ran. He got 10 yards without a hand being laid on him. He ran down the first foe in his way and ended up on the Ole Miss 30. The Rattlers did not cash the break, ending up with a third-down fumble, but the kick-run option threat had been established.

The Rattlers returned to plan A, first-down punts. The small, soaked crowd booed. Mitchell's aides questioned his strategy. Just run a couple of plays, they urged.

"This is my game," replied Mitchell. "You'll get your shot."

The tactics were not new. Mitchell had done the same thing in a Little Rock game, when his Arkansas team played Oklahoma State in a downpour. The coach theorized that such a game could be decided only by a turnover, probably a fumble. The odds were on his side, he felt, when his team punted on first down.

Even Mitchell began to question his strategy until finally Mississippi fumbled on its own eight-yard line with two minutes left in the first half. Three straight times fullback Bill Bovine bulled straight ahead, advancing the football to the two-yard line. Bill bulled again on fourth down. Only, he did not have the football. Quarterback Bobby Joe Jackson faked the handoff, and rolled right with ball hidden on hip. He scored without opposition. No human opposition, that is. The mud nearly got him. He went into a treacherous sideslip on the one-yard line, but put one hand down as an outrigger. He regained balance and lunged across the goal line. It was, as an old time public address announcer used to say, a case of near "self-tacklization." The extra point was kicked. Southwestern 7, Ole Miss 0 at halftime. A 7–0 lead is far from decisive. But it became inordinately important in these horrible conditions. Ole Miss felt compelled to gamble. An intercepted pass, caused when the Rattlers' crashing end deflected the ball, was converted into a 10-yard touchdown. Then, a fumble on the one set up another touchdown.

The Rattlers continued punting on first down. Frustrated Mississippi, a 12-point favorite, lost, 21–0.

The win was sweet, sweeter for me than most. Shirley Tate was in the press box. As a search committee member, she had put aside qualms about accepting favors from the athletic department, made the trip with the team and sat in the press box.

At game's end, she started jumping up and down. I felt compelled to explain to her that cheer-leading was not permitted in a press box. She shrugged, and threw her arms around me. She was warm and soft, as was the kiss she placed on my cheek.

CHAPTER 15

The Rattlers seemed to grow in the afterglow of that delightful dance in the Mississippi mud. Beating Nebraska was a larger upset but beating the Rebels was important. It proved the Nebraska win was no fluke. Thus validated, the Rattlers gained general acceptance, if not general adulation, in the Valley of the Sun.

Columnist Scoop Simon suggested in The Arizona Republic that reservations might become necessary for a seat on the Rattler band wagon, which fans were leaping aboard in droves.

Signs of the Rattlers' newly-found popularity popped up the minute the team charter plane landed in Phoenix. The Fossils had been unofficially adopted by radio station KOLD, which catered to the Geritol-for-lunch bunch. KOLD announced repeatedly that the team would arrive at Sky Harbor airport at 2:15 a.m. Sunday.

In a late gate-change, the officials had moved the Rattlers to Gate 21 in tribute to their score in Mississippi. Some 200 fans, all up hours beyond their usual bedtime, crowded around the gate to cheer the returning heroes.

The magnitude of the event was elevated a few notches by the unscheduled appearance of The Hot Flashes, a senior dance group used on commercials, in parades and at conventions. These ladies, all professional dancers in an earlier life, are eye catching, at least through bifocals. From their tiny skirts stretch some of the best legs on display at senior dances.

Players disembarked first from the chartered airplane, the six Football Fossils bringing up the rear. Say this for the Hot Flashes: They have a feel for the dramatic. They formed two lines and extended arms holding pom pons as far as they could reach. Created was a regal tunnel through which the smiling coaches exited. Well, it's the best they could do without swords.

The Hot Flashes led the crowd in a cheer, which was another clue to the age of the group.

"Two.four.six.eight.

Who do we appreciate?

Fossils, Fossils. Fossils."

That touched off a veritable avalanche of hype. Never had Southwestern wallowed in so much publicity. Talk shows were overrun by older fans, chortling over the success of the gridiron geezers.

Columnists wrote and announcers talked of the stunning start of the Fossils. The coaches themselves had opportunities to endorse everything from corn plasters to Grecian Formula—and to speak at civic clubs and to appear on television. Fan mail rolled in. Some offered romance to the Fossils.

Devine summarized the week: "Gee, it's hard to be humble."

It became harder. Coaches met every Monday morning at 9 a.m. to hear injury reports and make plans. The coach of the week presented his strategy. The other coaches tried to pick holes in it.

The meeting was interrupted by a polite knock on the door. It was opened to reveal erstwhile smartass Joe Fridena, who was to prove to be a pretty smart backup linebacker.

"Gentlemen, I'd like to say something," said Joe. "I wanted to apologize for what I said about you guys at the start. I was out of line. I want you to know I am privileged to be playing under all of you. And I think most of the guys on the team feel the same way. Thanks."

He quickly left, before it got too mushy. But what welcome words these were to the coaches. Acceptance by fans was unnecessary but acceptance of the players was vital.

Fortunately it was a bye week. Next game was on Nov. 1 at Texas. The time was needed to catch collective breaths and recover from all the attention.

• • •

There can be too much attention. The Rattler practice field was protected by a tall chain link fence, covered by ever-green foliage. Privacy was assured. At least that was the assumption until the Fossils had a visit from the assistant manager of a 10-story Marriott Hotel built a year ago two blocks from the practice facility.

It seems a big, brawny guy in cowboy boots had checked in on Tuesday and demanded a room on the top floor looking east onto the practice field. The man had registered from Boston but had a Texas twang. Maids said, when quizzed later, that he had a huge pair of binoculars.

It was after the guest left that the assistant manager added up facts and called on the Rattlers.

The unsubstantiated report was greeted with alarm. Coaches, paranoid souls that they are, always suspect spies are lurking in the woodwork. It was never substantiated that a Texas scout had spied from that 10th floor perch but the coaches were conditioned to expect the worse.

The Fossils felt action was required. But what kind? Should guards be hired? Could they buy out the east side of the 10th floor at the Marriott? Would helicopters spot spies? How about a powerful telescope for counter surveillance?

"Come on, men," said Darryl Rogers. "We're letting this get out of hand. All we have to do is run a 13-man defense."

The coaches nodded in unison. This was an old-time antidote for spying. Adding two too many defenders was sure to confuse spies. Which 11 of the 13 were real players and which were decoys? Without jersey numbers, which are rarely worn in practice, it was hard to know.

"Yeah," said Devine, "and why don't we give them something to look at with our offense. Let's put in some wishbone plays. Think that won't screw them up?"

So, the counter-espionage plot was set in motion. It was determined that the scout team, that is the one that normally runs opponents' plays in practice, would run the wishbone.

The wishbone, started to confuse spies, became a permanent addition to the repertoire. The Rattlers could use it, as did the Pittsburgh Steelers, in goal line situations.

The wishbone requires a special quarterback. The three options available to the wishbone quarterback are: (1) faking or handing off to the fullback running straight ahead, (2) keeping the football and cutting up field outside the tackle or (3) pitching out to a trailing halfback going wide. The quarterback needs to be athletic, quick to make decisions and have the ability to see the entire field. Such folks are hard to find. Right?

"No, not really," said Mitchell, the old quarterback. "It's just like the point guard in basketball."

Point guard. The designation rang a bell. A walkon, Jose Garcia, had been a good point guard. He was a good all-round athlete, and intelligent. Bingo. Jose was to be a good option quarterback. Better than good.

CHAPTER 16

Jose Garcia was a handsome, bronzed young man. Height: 6-foot-4. Weight: 216, all of it muscle. With his long, chiseled face and coal black hair, Jose resembled Roman Gabriel, a four-time pro bowl quarterback with the Los Angeles Rams. In appearance, that is. Not as a football player.

Jose was a starting point guard on the basketball team. He was agile and able to make accurate snap decisions. He had come out for football on a lark when the Fossils advertised for bodies. The worst he could do, Jose figured, was get a good seat for the football games and maybe wangle a trip to an away game. He, therefore, was totally unprepared when opportunity came a-knocking.

On the Wednesday following the Mississippi game, he was lolling around the sidelines when Chuck Fairbanks commanded, "Jose, get your helmet and get out here."

The Fossils required that everyone have a helmet on his head, in his hand or by his feet. The coaches wanted to develop in their players the habit of always being ready.

Jose, for all his endearing attributes, was not ready. He started looking for his helmet, finally locating it under the bench. He trotted out on the field with the helmet in hand. Suddenly, he stopped, looked down in his helmet, remembered and panicked. He hustled back to the sidelines, turned his helmet over—and out tumbled a bunch of nachos.

What the hell, he had decided, those marooned on the sidelines without specific duties needed nourishment.

The redeeming factor was that Jose knew more about quarterbacking than the coaches expected. He had been a backup quarterback in high school. He knew how to take the snap, how to hand off and how to call signals.

Jack Mitchell, designated option quarterback coach, took on Garcia as a personal project. Jose was intimidated by the multi-faceted requirements faced by the option quarterback.

"It's not all that tough," Mitchell told his young protégé. "You played point guard in basketball. Right?"

Without waiting for a reply, the coach continued. "The option play is just exactly like handling the ball on the two-on-one fast break. You have to keep the basketball or pass it off, depending on whether you are covered or the other guy is covered. It calls for a quick decision. But it's the same as the fast-break decision you've been making all your life."

Then, Mitchell took the fledgling quarterback onto the field. Mitchell play-acted the role of defensive end, rushing quickly to force a pitchout or laying back to encourage the run. Jose got the idea quickly. Then Mitchell added a fake. He faked a move toward the other guy, and then jumped back at the quarterback. The collision didn't exactly produce a mushroom cloud but was enough to stop practice. At season's end, Mitchell would enter Mayo's because of a bad back.

The bye before Texas enabled the Rattlers to stage a scrimmage on Saturday. The scouting team, running the wishbone, scrimmaged the varsity briefly. Garcia took a lot of knocks, but no knockouts. He bounced up from each blow more quickly than the guy who decked him. Encouraging.

On Tuesday, some muscle was added to the scout team, when it was joined by two of the Rattlers' most talented subs. One was a left halfback, Rashad Moshier, who was quick as a blink. Another was Bill Bovine's younger brother, Bob, a fearless 221-pound fullback who could block.

It became obvious that the scout team was capable of running a few wishbone plays against Texas as a surprise changeup. Capable enough, at least, to earn their own nickname, "The Boners."

Question: How did this addition of the wishbone sit with Fairbanks, the Fossils coach of the week? Answer: It was fine and dandy. Fairbanks had been through the same switch once before. And against Texas. And, with good long-range results.

Fairbanks was elevated to head coach at Oklahoma in 1967 following the death of Jim Mackenzie. He got the job by presidential decree. Dr. George L. Cross, president of the university, picked him. The Board of Regents, outraged at being bypassed, ratified the move but stipulated the contract was only for one year.

After his first team went 10–1, Fairbanks was embraced by regents as permanent coach. And, lived happily ever after? No, not quite.

In those days, Oklahoma fans were the most rabid and unreasonable supporters on this planet. Season tickets could be had only through wills of deceased fans. Many of the faithful decreed that their ashes be scattered over Owen Field, even though said remains would be picked up from the Astroturf by a vacuum cleaner.

Among sportswriters, the Oklahoma fans were known as "The Chinamen." Once upon a time, a visiting writer was appalled to see the Oklahoma fans calling for more touchdowns even though their team was leading by three touchdowns. The writer's lead was: "How much rice can a Chinaman eat?"

Fairbanks was not cradled to the Chinamen's bosom—mainly because his teams lost four straight games to Texas, the Sooners most hated rival. Bumper stickers appeared: "Send Fairbanks Back to Alaska."

The fourth loss of the series was a back-breaker. In that 1970 Texas game, Fairbanks switched to the wishbone. Writers laughed and fans booed. This was ridiculous. Fairbanks was springing the wishbone on Texas, the team that had popularized the formation. Might as well enter a bakeoff with Betty Crocker.

The Sooners had worked on the wishbone during a bye week. It was, as one would expect, no match for the Texas' wishbone. The Longhorns won 41–7.

But this game was a Sooner watershed, and Oklahoma was the long-range winner. The wishbone fit the Sooner talent. The quick halfbacks and nifty quarterbacks were ideal for the option attack.

How ideal? Well, Oklahoma was to lose only eight of its next 66 games. Only one season after adopting the wishbone, Oklahoma was involved in the best college game ever played.

Nebraska was rated No.1 nationally and Oklahoma No.2 when the titans met on Thanksgiving Day of 1971. This was a rare instance when the game matched the buildup. Nebraska won, 35–31 but no one lost. It was simply that Nebraska had last bats. In the final poll, Nebraska was No. 1, Oklahoma No. 2. And No.3 was Colorado, another Big Eight power which had lost only to Nebraska and Oklahoma.

In a post-game party after the Nebraska classic, Fairbanks was asked if this was the biggest game in which he had been involved.

"The biggest since Charlevoix played East Jordan," he deadpanned.

Nice thought. Bigness, he was saying, is in the eye of the beholder. If those involved truly care, a high school game in Michigan can be as big as a collegiate championship game.

Fairbanks was a good end at Charlevoix. East Jordan was coached by a rookie named Dan Devine. Both ended up at Michigan State, Devine as a student assistant and Fairbanks as a player. A Spartan standout at about the same time was still a third Fossil, Frank Kush. Strange how paths converge in athletics.

Alas, we wander. The point is, Fairbanks remembered Texas and the wishbone. Both dramatically impacted his career.

It's amazing how a couple of unexpected victories can wake up the citizenry. Sun Devil stadium, rarely more than half full for the Rattlers' games, held nearly 50,000 for the Texas game.

Trick plays had become a Fossil trademark. The Dirty Trick guys, one visiting writer called them. And a Dirty Trick file had been started. It was stocked by the Fossils, their coaching friends and even by fans' mail-in suggestions. At that juncture, the file contained some 50 trick plays.

Some, granted, were too wild even for the nothing-to-lose interim coaches. For instance, one was the kickoff huddle, supposedly used in early times by legendary Pop Warner. On the kickoff, the kick receiver joined the other 10 men to form a huddle at about the 20-yard line. Each player spun out of the huddle in a different direction. They hunched over, so that the opposition could not determine which of the 11 had the football. According to lore, Warner had footballs painted onto the belly of the team jerseys to add to the confusion.

This one was too far out even for the Fossils. But, convinced that early trickery could swing momentum, they decided on another gimmick play—The Mickey Mouse kickoff return, popularized by Oklahoma State.

The Rattlers won the coin toss, and received. J. J. Hunker took the football a yard deep in the endzone and raced straight up the field. The wedge had formed at the 20-yard line. Hidden behind it, facing toward the onrushing Hunker , was quarterback Jose Garcia. Hunker slipped the ball into Garcia's midsection as he ran past. Meanwhile circling from the left side of the formation was speed-merchant Rashad Smith. Without missing a step, he fielded the lateral from Garcia and dashed to the sideline.

Kickoff coverage teams are trained to stay in lanes, covering the breadth of the field. But the sight of Hunker bolting up the middle had lured the coverage to him. It was cakewalk for Smith. No one touched him.

Scoop Simon got carried away a bit, writing: "Maybe the Hunker to Garcia to Moshier magic wasn't a match for baseball's Tinkers to Evers to Chance but it was football's reasonable replica."

A game winner? Maybe against a lesser foe but Texas was not to yield easily—not with a quarterback like Billy Bob Jacobsen. He engineered an 80-yard march, hitting on 4 of 5 passes for 66 yards, to tie the score at 7–7. A fumble on the kickoff, and a 17-yard pass, put Texas ahead, 14–7.

Gulp. What we had here was a gut check. Southwestern quarterback Bobby Joe Jackson responded with a 63-yard drive mixing the blasts of Bill Bovine and his own passing. Score: 14–14.

And that's how it went. Touchdowns were almost as frequent as first downs. Heads swiveled. You would have thought it was a tennis match. Texas led 24–21 at halftime.

And what, you may ask, happened to the seven diamond defense that Southwestern used to virtually shut down Nebraska and Mississippi? Well, it developed later, that Texas had acquired film of an early Nebraska game in which the Huskers solved the Missouri seven diamond by using abbreviated rollouts, or a moving pocket as Coach Hank Stram once named it.

The movement of the quarterback slowed the onrushing defensive end and kept the one linebacker from dropping back in pass coverage.

Texas used the strategy to open up passes into the flanks and up the middle to the tight end. Efforts to plug those holes made it easier for wide receivers to streak down the sideline.

The Rattlers' Jackson was matching his Texas foe pass for pass but sorely needed some kind of rushing game. The Rattlers had delayed using their wishbone until the second half, so Texas could not design a defense for it during intermission. The worst that could happened, reasoned the Fossil braintrust, was that it would give future foes something to think about.

Jose Garcia could have choked but didn't. Basketball had built a mental toughness in this young man. He had only three plays that could be run in either direction—(1) give to the fullback, (2) keep off tackle or (3) pitch to the tailback. Ideally, the quarterback deals off the football according to how the defense reacts. If the hole for the fullback is plugged, the quarterback proceeds down the line toward the keeper. If that is well defended, he tosses off to the trailing tailback.

In this instance, however, the option was taken out of the option play. To ease the load on the quarterback, the Rattlers pre-determined which option would be exercised. But the Longhorns did not realize that.

Bovine rammed for two yards on the first play. Garcia pitched to left halfback Rashad Moshier on the second play. It went for 18 yards. Only a fine open field tackle by the Texas safetyman kept it from going all the way. No matter. The Boners scored in six plays, for a 28–24 lead.

The wishbone, by and large, had been in mothballs for a decade, except for service schools. The wishbone had faded when opponents learned it could be stopped with an eight-man front, but Texas was reluctant to change from its basic 4–3–4 defense.

The Rattler wishbone wasn't, from a technical standpoint, all that good. But the surprise element made it look good. To keep Texas guessing, the Rattlers alternated attacks—the pro set with Jackson and the wishbone with Garcia.

Still it wasn't easy. Quarterback Billy Bob Jacobsen was having a great day for Texas. The Rattlers' 42-38 lead seemed insecure when the Longhorns drove to a first down on the Southwestern two-yard line with 1:42 remaining.

Fairbanks had been there before. Nebraska had beaten his Oklahoma team in that classic 1971 game by having the ball last. Rehashes of the game brought up another strategic possibility for Oklahoma then. Now, it was used against Texas.

The Rattlers let Texas score, stepping out of the way as Billy Bob sneaked in. The Longhorn fans could not believe what their eyes saw. They arose, cheering the benevolence of the foe's defense.

There was method in the apparent madness. Southwestern was conceding the touchdown quickly to save time on the clock. Mike Holmgren, Green Bay Packer coach, had used the same tactic unsuccessfully in the 1998 Super Bowl loss to Denver.

With 1:06 and two timeouts left, the Rattlers started from their own 34-yard line. A surprise draw play to Bill Bovine gained 11 yards.

With the Texas secondary crowding the sideline, the Rattlers pulled out the old hook-and-lateral trick. Jackson fired a hook pass to tight end Kent Winters, who was spotted up in a vacant middle area eight yards deep. The defense converged on Winters as he caught the football. Winters then lateralled to trailing halfback, Rashad Moshier. Only a desperate tackle by the Texas safety on the Texas 40-yard line saved a touchdown. Another draw play failed to catch the Longhorns out of position. Bill Bovine gained two yards and a time-out had to be used.

A second straight draw caught Texas in an all-out pass rush. Bovine gained seven yards to the 31, but the clock ticked off 22 seconds before Jackson could get his troops in place. The quarterback then sneaked one yard for a clock-stopping first down. Relentlessly, the clock had ticked down to 10 seconds.

Jackson was great in these situations. "Plenty of time, guys," he told the players in the huddle. "No need to get excited. Relax. Do your job. That's all we need."

Again, Jackson passed to the uncrowded middle, hitting Jones Keith for nine yards to the 21. The last time out was used to stop the clock with 5 seconds left.

From his own bag of Dirty Tricks, Fairbanks unearthed the same play which had allowed Alabama to tie Oklahoma in the 1970 Bluebonnet Bowl game. The play call was signaled into Jackson.

Jackson pitched out to halfback Tim Pruitt running to his right. As Pruitt cocked his arm to pass, Texas who had every receiver covered— every one except the quarterback. Jackson stood alone on the far sideline. He had to wait an eternity for Pruitt's long lob. But the quarterback, unaccustomed though he was to receiving passes, hauled it in easily. Jackson left the only opponent with a shot at him grabbing a big bunch of nothing. He scored.

Southwestern won, 49–45, in a shootout that stood the Valley of the Sun on its ear.

CHAPTER 17

Herman Hickman, one-time coach and resident sage at Yale, once said, "The successful football coach is the one who can appear to be leading a parade while being chased out of town."

Success becomes such a difficult term to define in this era of exaggerated expectations. Winning is not enough. Wins also are graded on style points. A team must look good winning. And also beat the point spread. Even winning coaches are criticized.

The thought arose while listening to a talk show in which irate customers found a way to knock the Fossils, even though gridiron's golden boys were 3–0 against top-notch opponents.

KTAR, which carries the Rattler games on radio, stages a weekly call-in show. The talk show is hosted by Hedrick Thomas, better known as "The Parrot" because he can mimic anybody or because he rattles on forever or both.

The latter trait proved useful. The Parrot sometimes is forced into a monologue because Fossil appearances on the hour-long talk show are spasmodic. The coaches, according to the original agreement, appeared only if they felt like it.

That's an option any coach would relish. Bad hair day. Sorry, Hedrick I won't be there. Hey, Hedrick, get a sub. I've got a round of golf.

On this night, the Parrot had both Chuck Fairbanks, who had coached the previous week, and Frank Kush, who was to coach the next game against Arizona.

The Parrot introduced the first caller as Tom from Sun City. Said Tom, "Every Phoenix resident, not just retirees, should stand and applaud you super senior coaches. You have given us three great wins. Exciting wins. You have attracted national attention. Thanks, guys."

The next three callers continued along these same effusive lines, leaving the coaches muttering, "Aw shucks, 'tweren't nothing." Or something like that.

But caller No. 5 was an unexpected departure.

Said Bob from Glendale: "Everybody's raving about you coaches, but the fact is you should have won that Texas game easily and by more than four points."

Kush fielded this one. "What was the point spread?"

"Five points," said the caller.

"And how much did you lose?" Kush asked.

"That's not the point."

"Oh, yes it is." Kush's voice rose a few decibels. There was a cutting edge to his words. "That's exactly the point. And I'll tell you this, the day we start playing to cover the spread is the day college football, as we know it, dies. Sure, there are a lot of things wrong in college football but playing to satisfy the gamblers is not one of them."

Tom in Queen Creek called with ire in his voice. "This Rattler staff is supposed to be so smart. If you are, how come you don't pick this up: Do you know that quarterback, that Billy Joe Jackson, tips it off every time he's going to pass by licking his fingers?" "Yes, we are aware of that," said Fairbanks. "We are also are aware that he licks his fingers before every play."

Three laudatory calls followed before another hostile voice was heard.

Said Albert from Tempe: "You guys make me sick. Everybody's worshipping at that senior citizen shrine. Heroes, you ain't. What you are is washed-up has-beens who are working only because Boots Anderson was railroaded out of there.

"Anybody who knows anything about football knows the wishbone formation and the seven-diamond defense went out with leather helmets."

There was a pregnant pause, broken eventually by the calm voice of Fairbanks. "And what is your coaching experience, sir? At what level did you coach? How and where did you get your vast football experience."

Replied Albert, "That has nothing do with it, but I was once a Pop Warner coach, and I played some high school football."

"On which end of the bench did you sit, sir?"

Replied Albert, "My experience is not the issue. The way you over-aged coaches coach is."

"Sorry, but experience is a factor," said Fairbanks. "Do you mean to tell me a guy coaching one year of kids football knows as much about the game as six coaches with more than a combined 100 years as head coaches in college? Here's another stat. Combined, we guys have coached more than 1,000 college games and won over 60 per cent of them."

"Maybe that's the problem," said Albert. "You know too much. Hell, you can't run the stuff you have and you still keep sticking in that weirdo stuff—onside kicks, screwball returns on kickoffs, punt-run options. Next thing you know you'll be putting in the single wing."

Kush laughed out loud. "We are thinking about putting in the single wing. What you don't grasp, even with all your Pop Warner experience, is that we have managed to use up much of the opponents' practice time with those "weirdo" things. No coach can ignore the gimmick plays we use. They have to at least expose their team to the possibilities.

"By the way, how much time do you spend looking at Rattler film?"

Albert spoke with a little more confidence. "As a matter of fact I video tape the Sunday night replay and go through it at least three times to grade all the players. And it gives me an idea which plays to call. "

"Three times," said Kush. "Boy, that must be a thorough report. Maybe you'd be interested in knowing our coaches dissect each play by running and re-running it 10 or 15 times

"And the big difference is they know what they're looking for. No way can you grade a cornerback unless you know which of our six defensive alignments we're using and what his assignment is.

"And play calling? Hell, we have at least 10 films on each opponent. And we re-run them a dozen times. Computers are used to figure out tendencies. We know what play an opponent is likely to run in any situation—taking in consideration the field position, down and distance.

"You don't have films of opponents or computer tendencies, sir, but you think you can call plays better than we can.

"I get sick of people who grade football on style points. You want to know how to grade coaches? Just add up wins and losses. We haven't had any losses yet, if I remember correctly."

Albert hung up.

The last caller was a fellow who sounded more than slightly inebriated. His name came out with an indecipherable slur. "What's faster. a elephant or a hippo?"

Fairbanks shrugged. He didn't know. Neither did Kush. The Parrot said, "Sorry, sir, we don't have the answer."

"Dats okay," said the caller. "We got 'em here in the livin room. We'll jus race 'em and find out."

For Kush and Fairbanks, the ride home was light and cheery. There was no sign of the anger lingering from the Fossil critics. A long-festering frustration had been wiped out.

"God, that was fun," said Kush. "I've always wanted to tell off one of those idiot know-it-alls."

CHAPTER 18

The overflow turnout at Sun Devil Stadium for the Southwestern-Arizona game was not surprising. Not if you consider all the turn-ons involved in this, the second coming of Frank Kush.

Kush, the Rattlers' head coach for the week, is turned on by the UofA. And the state is turned on by Kush.

Biggest turn-on, however, was the nostalgia and irony of the situation. Here was Kush, a fallen hero making a triumphant return to a field which now bears his name.

With this stage setting, the Rattler-Wildcat contest, heretofore a ho-hum affair, became the biggest draw of the season at Sun Devil stadium. Official count was 74,130, which was 769 more than the listed capacity. Emotions ran high. Banners and signs decorated the premises.

"Welcome Home Frank."

"Wake Up The Echoes."

"Frankly, We Missed You"

Kush is tough and he's demanding. Play your butt off for him and he loved you, although he rarely showed it. Play less than your best and you'd see his growling face in your face, or feel his boot in your butt or his hand shaking the cage on the front of your helmet.

Fans loved it. At least they loved his success. How, pray tell, would anyone dare to criticize a guy whose Arizona State teams were 176–54–1 over 22 years. His ASU teams won nine conference championships and were 6–1 in bowls. He had 38 All Americans and 128 players drafted into professional football.

A coach like that will take a lot of forgiving, particularly in a frontier state. As an old-fashioned disciplinarian, Kush had not kept up with newfangled player relations philosophy. Coaches now come wearing velvet gloves, not boxing gloves. The hands-on approach is frowned on. Now, players are smothered with praise not cussed with a scowl.

Kush's son, Danny, kicked three field goals including the game-winner, in a landmark 17–14 victory over Nebraska in the 1975 Fiesta Bowl. ASU wound up 12-0 and the second ranked team in the nation.

A reporter suggested that the biggest problem for Kush in having son Danny on the team was that the coach was unable to praise son when he performed well. Was that a problem for Kush? "Naw," he growled. "I never praised anyone, anyway."

Veteran Phoenix sports writer Jacob Robertson twice was kicked out of the locker room by Kush.

"Win or lose, it didn't matter, Frank was always the same, a jerk," said Robertson. "But we now have become good friends."

On a slow day, a television cameraman could always catch Kush kicking ass or rattling a helmet. It was after such a episode had been splashed over local TV screens that Kush met with an assortment of visiting sports writers.

It was a touching scene, one of the few times Kush endeavored to explain himself. He told how he grew up with tough love and tough discipline. His dad whipped him and the nuns at school cracked his knuckles with a ruler when he misbehaved. That wasn't punishment, he suggested. That was how life was.

Afterwards, I suggested to Kush that it would all blow over. "No it won't," he said.

A day later, a lawsuit against Kush was announced. A punter named Kevin Rutledge charged in a civil suit that Kush had punched him when he came off the field after a bad punt in a game a year earlier at the University of Washington.

The civil suit later was dismissed and an appeal failed. Decisive? Possibly, but by then it was a classic case of too little, too late.

The walls came tumbling down on Kush with startling speed on October 13, 1971. That was the evening on which Arizona State was to play Washington. Kush had inklings of what was to come a day earlier but it was on game day he got official word—brought rather surprisingly by an assistant coach who informed Kush that he was to be dismissed. The assistant said he had been alerted to take over the head coaching duties for the Washington game.

The decision apparently had been made by Fred Miller, the athletic director, with the approval of the university president. They planned to accuse Kush of trying to cover up the Rutledge affair by coercing assistants to lie on his behalf.

Kush simply ignored the second-hand instructions delivered by his assistant to step down. Frank Kush was not to be railroaded that easily. He reported at the stadium as he normally would, went through his usual pre-game routine and coached the game. My, how he coached. A 12–7 upset of Washington was Kush's going-away present.

Word of his impending ouster had swept like wildfire through the community all day Saturday. Irate Kush supporters arrived early. They came with banners, signs and loud, angry voices.

The coach was welcomed with a standing ovation. Kush would have won a public opinion poll hands down. The outpouring was unprecedented. With any kind of encouragement, a lynch mob could have been formed that night to confront the ASU brass. Fast forward to September 21, 1996. Nebraska was the foe. The Huskers were top ranked, winner of the national championship the past two years. But Arizona State again was the upset winner, 19–0, touching off a march into the Rose Bowl.

Kush obviously was not the coach against Nebraska. But he was present and his presence was felt.

It was Frank Kush night. The field was dedicated as Kush Field. A statue of Kush was unveiled before 200 of his former players. And a $3 million endowment bearing Kush's name was announced.

Nice touch, huh? All this for a coach that ASU, in effect, had run off 15 years earlier. The larger-than-life-size statue of Kush stands at the south entrance to the stadium. At the dedication, one-time ASU quarterback Danny White walked over and kicked the rear of the statue. "Yeah, that's Frank," he said. "Still a hard ass."

Was Kush really all that tough? Certainly not around kids, particularly the kids of his assistant coaches. Frank loved to tell them stories. And he listened to them intently, as if truly interested in their thoughts.

But, yes, Kush was tough. As our last witness to that fact, let's call in Reggie Jackson, Hall of Fame baseball great who came to ASU on a football scholarship.

"I'll always be indebted to Frank Kush for instilling toughness in his players," Jackson has said. "He was as tough as Charlie Finley and George Steinbrenner rolled up in one."

CHAPTER 19

What retired coaches miss most, it has been alleged, is the attention. Certainly the return to celebrity status was a joy for the Fossils. The gridiron grandpas went instantly from forgotten men to heroes—particularly in the media.

The media darling was Kush. Why not? Here was a legendary coach returning to a field named for him, one on which he had been honored, dishonored and honored again.

"What was his most significant game in 22 years at Arizona State?" Kush was asked. He mulled it over. There were several possibilities.

Old-timers would have picked the "Ultimatum Bowl" of 1968. Arizona was 8–1 and ASU 7–2 going into their game. A Sun Bowl bid awaited the winner.

Darrell Mudra, the Arizona coach, forced the issue. Take us before the game, he told the Sun Bowl, or you won't get us. The Sun Bowl caved in and took Arizona. Fired up by the slight, ASU beat Arizona, 30–7, and touched off a drive which would lead to formation of the Fiesta Bowl.

Many consider that the most pivotal game in ASU history was the 1975 Fiesta Bowl in which ASU upset favored Nebraska, 17–14. Never had the national spotlight shined so brightly on the Sun Devils. They wound up No. 2 in national ratings.

Kush's somewhat-surprising answer, however, was that he considered the most significant game in his reign not the 1975 Fiesta Bowl, but the game that preceded it. That was a nail-biting game with Arizona. Without the 24–21 victory in that one, ASU would not have been in the Fiesta Bowl. "One of the better games I was ever involved with," said Kush. "Both teams were extremely talented. A lot of the players from that game went into the pro game."

From that game, Kush exhumed two plays for the Rattlers to use against Arizona in the current game. One was the "Z" pass pattern run twice by legendary wide receiver John Jefferson. Another was the draw play, with a delayed fuse, on which Fast Freddie Williams twice gained good yardage. The double draw, it was called.

Another hunk of history was used for openers of the Arizona Southwestern game. Since its beginning, Southwestern had been bugged by a lady named Lenora Leonard. She wanted to sing the National Anthem in the pre-game ceremonies.

Why Southwestern moguls took this occasion to grant her wish will forever remain a mystery.

Ms. Leonard said she had operatic training. If so, it was as a stage-hand, which she closely resembled. Time had eroded her pitch, plus her memory.

Two hours before kickoff, she took a big gulp of her medicinal bourbon to subdue the nervous shakes. It didn't help much. Still leery, she filled an old Hadacol bottle with more bourbon. She took it with her to the press box, and started nipping again an hour before kickoff.

Ms. Leonard was sober enough to realize her mind was not working well. As a safeguard, she scribbled the words to the the Star Spangled Banner on 3-by-5 cards.

She then was escorted to midfield, and instructed to face the west stands where the dignitaries were located. The house light dimmed. Hell, they all were turned off. Only light in the place was the spotlight that shined in Ms. Leonard's eyes from the west stands.

The band started but Ms. Leonard didn't. The one spotlight left her crib notes in the dark. The band re-started. Ms. Leonard, bless her heart, pulled out a cigarette lighter and read the words from its light.

"Oh say can you see by the dawn's early light."

Prophetic words. The light from Ms. Leonard's Zippo caught her notes on fire. As they burned away, she hummed through the rest of the anthem.

Never has the National Anthem evoked so many laughs. What would Kush do for an encore?

As a matter of fact, he did pretty well. As a guest on a talk-show, Kush was needled by a caller named Albert.

"Fossil thinking was outmoded," said Albert. He sneered and laughed simultaneously. "Next thing you know, you has-beens will put in the single wing."

"Maybe we will," said Kush, more to needle the needler than to endorse the single wing. It was only later that Kush decided it might be fun to run a few single wing plays.

So he did. The scout team, also known as the Boners because it introduced the wishbone, was picked to run the ancient single wing formation. The football antique was turned over to the subs so as not to waste the valuable time of the regulars.

It started as a practical joke, an adventure to enliven practice. No one figured the formation would be carried beyond the practice field. The scout team had only three plays, all from single wing right. They could run the off-tackle play, the sweep and one other play.

Most of the scout team backfield adapted well to the single wing. Quarterback Jose Garcia was the only shaky fit. The quarterback in the single wing is a blocking back who lines up behind his tackle. Rashad Moshier had the size and speed to play tailback. Bob Bovine was ideal as the fullback. The wingback, who lines up outside the offensive end, was swift Patrick Young.

On the first play against Arizona, the scout team lined up in single wing right.

Garcia had lined up under the tackle, not under center as he would normally in the T formation. He stuck his hands between the tackle's legs as if to take the center snap. Then Jose looked around, puzzled.

To the tackle, Martin Joseph, Garcia said loudly, "What the hell are you doing centering the ball?"

This little wrinkle, worked out by the players themselves, left the Arizona defense doubled up in mirth. At that point, the Rattlers could have run anything successfully. The Arizona defense was back on its heels.

The ball was snapped deep to Smith. He hammered off right tackle, where double-team blocks wiped out the unprepared end and tackle. Bovine leveled the linebacker. The play, to the surprise of all, broke Rashad wide open. Speed was all he had. Speed was all he needed. He sped 76 yards and suddenly, with the crowds still filing in, the Rattlers had a 7–0 lead.

Once again, the Rattlers' gimmickry left an opponent somewhat tentative, waiting for the next cleated shoe to drop.

Arizona coaches later confided the halftime was wasted trying to explain the single wing, and how to defend against it.

Rod Norman, the Rattlers' soccer-type kicker from Australia, toed the kickoff following the single-wing touchdown. The football bounced around as if making its way through a pinball machine and wound up in the iron mitts of an Arizona tackle, Albert Padilla, who had dropped back to the 25-yard line to be part of the blocking wedge.

What happened was predictable. Padilla couldn't hold onto anything, aside from his girl friend. He dropped the bouncing football. Southwestern recovered on the Arizona 25-yard line.

Arizona's limited research of Rattler tendencies indicated Southwestern was likely to go for a homerun after turnovers. So sure were the Wildcats that they inserted a fifth defensive back in the place of a linebacker.

A perfect setup, this, for one of the trick plays Kush had resurrected from the 1975 game with Arizona. It was the draw play, with a delayed fuse.

The draw in itself is a delay play. The quarterback retreats as if to pass, but slips the ball into the gut of a running back, who delays until defenders, in pursuit of the apparent passer, go past him. For Arizona in 1975, Kush designed the double delay draw for Fast Freddie Williams.

It was a normal draw, except that Williams delayed not one second but three. To himself, Freddie counted, "Thousand one, thousand two, thousand three."

The resurrected version featured Tailback Tim Pruitt, who delayed for the full three seconds, which seemed a lifetime. But during that time the rushing Arizona linemen sped past him. Pruitt exploded up the middle. He side-stepped a safetyman 10 yards downfield, and cruised 25 yards into the endzone. Less than two minutes into the game, the Rattlers had a 14–0 lead.

It was too easy too soon. The Rattlers settled back into their we've-got-it-won stance only to be awakened to reality on the last play of the first half. The Rattler receivers had success by faking in, and then darting to the outside. They did it once too often. Arizona cornerback Jeff Vann stepped in front of the Rattlers' Jones Keith, neatly fielded the pass and raced 47 yards for an Arizona score.

The holder for the extra point, sub quarterback Jim Thomas, was careful not to put his knee on the ground. He rolled out as the kicker faked the kick and managed to run around the hard rush. Arizona was back in the game although behind, 14–8.

The in-out pass pattern which led to the key interception was used to start the second half—but with one change. One more move was added to produce what Kush called a "Z' pattern. It was originally put in for John Jefferson in the 1975 Arizona game. It required time. The receiver had to fake in, fake out and then cut in over the middle. The Rattlers kept everyone in to block except Jones Keith.

Keith faked in, then out. He later said Vann's mouth watered, seeing the play come his way again. But the third cut, back toward the middle, left Vann immobilized. Keith pulled in the pass and easily won a 65-yard foot race. Score: Southwestern 21, Arizona 8.

Southwest then went for the jugular, with an onside kick attempt following the touchdown. Alert by now to trickery, Arizona recovered on their own 40 and marched 60 yards on five plays to again move within range at 21–15.

In the middle of the fourth quarter, Aussie Rod Norman did what coaches had been fearing. His low, hard punt went straight into the hands of the Arizona punt returner, the cornerback Vann. The returner had a full head of speed before he encountered opposition. He sidestepped one foe and stiff armed another en route to a 73-yard touchdown.

Suddenly, Arizona was ahead, 22–21.

Say this for the Rattler staff. It had guts. Granted that courage comes more easily when your job is not on the line. Still, they surprised everyone by throwing their subs, the scout team, back into this tight, see-sawing affair with three minutes remaining. Furthermore, the subs returned to the antiquated single wing.

At halftime, Arizona defensive coaches set up a overly-simplified solution for the single wing. They essentially committed 10 of their defenders to plug the off-tackle and sweep holes. They were warned to knock down blockers if they couldn't knock down the ball carrier. The outside right linebacker was cautioned to stay home to guard against a wingback reverse.

The single wing often was criticized as being unimaginative. Nonsense. Nothing was more imaginative than the buck-lateral series, a standard in most single-wing attacks. It worked perfectly in this crucial situation.

In the single wing, two men are in position to take a direct center snap—the tailback and the fullback, who is a step closer and a step to the side of the tailback.

The snap went directly to fullback Bob Bovine, who bolted straight at tackle. Quarterback Jose Garcia was stationed behind the tackle. At the snap, Garcia turned to face the onrushing Bovine, who stuck the football in the quarterback's gut. In the meantime, tailback Rashad Moshier was circling right far beyond the traffic jam at tackle and end. Garcia made a underhanded lateral pass to Moshier. He encountered absolutely no opposition in going 62 yards to the winning touchdown. With the run, Southwestern won, 28–22. Arizona was handed only its second loss of the season.

In the post-game press conference, Kush said, "If anyone knows a talk-show caller named Albert, tell him to give me another call."

CHAPTER 20

After the victory over Arizona in their home finale, the Fossils were invited to a post-game party by the Southwestern president, Dr. Justin White. They would have preferred their normal celebrations with brats and beer at one of the coaches' homes. Instead, they got those tiny cucumber sandwiches, broccoli to dip and champagne to sip.

The snooty food was a good match for the snooty crowd of 30 well-heeled alums, 29 of whom considered themselves expert critics of football.

Well-heeled alums, someone once said, were like a bunch of pissants on a log floating down a river. "Everyone of those pissants thinks he's guiding the log," said the philosopher.

The least snooty of the lot was Dr. White. He had adapted remarkably well to the rugged, free-wheeling, hard-living style of the desert, considering he had spent most of his first 50 years in mid-America, living largely in hallowed halls of learning.

Dr. White was bright. It took him less than a month to figure out that longevity in his new position depended on his ability to raise money, and that the big donors were those who doted on football. So, Dr. White became one of them.

He also dressed to fit the environment. He wore jeans to work. Formal attire included a string tie through a white collar tipped with silver. For major events, he added a western jacket with a lot of stitching on the pockets. He wore cowboy boots, which went much better in the feed lots than the penny loafers with which he arrived.

He usually wore a leather vest. That may have been carryback to his old three-piece suits but more likely was part of the wardrobe because it was a handy place to hang his watch chain, from which dangled his Phi Beta Kappa key.

Only in architecture did Dr. White fail to adapt to his surroundings. Arizona homes come in adobe, or stucco or slump bricks. Dr. White's house was the exact replica, at the insistence of wife Eleanor, of her family's home in Virginia. It was a white clapboard colonial. It was beautiful but completely out of place—like an anchovy atop a ice cream sundae.

White's White House, it was called. Perhaps it was reverse snobbery, but the Fossils did not feel at home with the White house, or with the guests inside it on this night.

The Fossils had been sheltered from irate alums, that being a stipulation of their original agreement. But here, among the wealthy wine-sippers, they were subjected to the same kind of nonsense most coaches must endure regularly.

One guest wanted to know where the single wing came from. Another asked why Kush had the tailback sit still so long before he took off on that draw play.

But the most obnoxious second-guesser was a personal injury attorney. P. N. Butts was his name. His biggest problem was that he believed what the yellow pages and TV ads said about him.

He blurted out, as if facing a jury, "What the hell I want explained to me is this: Why would any idiot run an onside kick with a two-touchdown lead?"

"Well, the surprise element..." That's as far as Al Onofrio got before Butts interrupted.

"And why would you let a guy like that Arizona holder fake you out for two points?"

Kush started to answer, but Butts held up a hand to stop him and continued the Q-A session without the A.

"Why don't you teach that damned Aussie punter to get a punt up instead of kicking those line drives? For a bunch of supposedly experienced and successful coaches, you guys pull a bunch of lulus."

The outburst was greeted with silence. It was obvious the lawyer had amply satisfied his thirst, if not his ego. The host didn't know whether to ignore him, or give him another drink.

But Dan Devine, normally a mild-mannered sort, felt an answer was required.

"And what, Mr. Butts, is your profession?" he asked.

"I'm a lawyer, sir."

"Oh yes," Devine said. "I've seen your ads. And I have a few questions for you. Is it now ethical for lawyers to advertise? How come legal fees are so high? Why do they need retainers? If we got rid of frivolous litigation, how many lawyers would have to look for a real job? And why, pray tell, do lawyers take six typewritten pages to say what any normal person could say in half a page? Why are lawyers always late? Do they think they're doctors, or what?"

Devine paused to catch his breath. Given the opportunity, Butts stuck his quickly-reddening face in the coach's face.

"Please tell me, Mr. Devine, how you became such an expert on the legal profession?"

Dan smiled. "The same way you became such an expert on football coaching."

Dr. White stepped between the two, as a referee might separate two fighters, and announced that he needed to consult privately with the coaches. He led the six into his den.

"I intended to ask you coaches to help us raise money from these folks."

Greeted by angry frowns, Dr. White quickly backpedaled.

"Loosen up, guys. That was a joke. I know our original agreement keeps us from asking you to raise funds or recruit. But I would like to impose on you in another area.

"Gentlemen, I want you to know that we deeply appreciate what you have done. We'd love it if you'd stick around. We know that is not possible. But we have been impressed with your knowledge of the game and of the people associated with it.

"We therefore want to ask for your assistance in one chore which will have a huge impact on our football future. We want you, all six of you, to act as a screening committee for our next coach. Our people will do the preliminary work and give you half a dozen possibilities. You would not be limited to those, however. We want to be certain we have a coach who knows football, knows how to get along with people and has good intelligence and good moral values. We feel you can make good judgments in this area, or at least know people who can make those judgments."

No answer was necessary. It was obvious the coaches were willing to help. It's flattering to be asked to pick your own successor.

"One more thing," said White. "We want the mechanics of this search to be as simple as possible. Shirley Tate will be chairman of the regular search committee, and will pick representatives from the faculty, student body and alumni. She will explain to her committee that the current coaching staff has the final word.

"We are making Bull Bullington the liaison between Ms. Tate and the coaches. We know they work well together."

I could have kissed him. Instead, I ended up kissing Shirley Tate, who was a far more desirable target than the president.

Shirley and I crossed paths frequently, and I often gave her a lift home or joined her for a cocktail. But on this night I crossed a threshold, hers. She invited me into her fifth-floor apartment for coffee.

I was extremely well behaved, largely because I had trouble believing anyone as young and beautiful as Shirley Tate would have any romantic interest in anyone as old and decrepit as me. I became a believer that night. Upon taking my leave, I kissed her on her cheek, which was normal under such circumstances.

She looked at me and grinned. "Don't you know where my lips are?"

With that, she gave me a peck, right on my lips.

I didn't need the elevator. I just floated down.

CHAPTER 21

A brush fire threatened the Rattlers' practice field. Actually, it was a small fire, more suited for marshmallows than headlines. But the eager press corps now hovering around the Rattlers made the bonfire seem to be a major conflagration. Thus was the newly-found popularity of the Rattlers validated.

The Fossils were unbeaten in four games and the team was 8-1, and rated 13th in the national polls. Reporters doted on the Rattlers every move, every word. A hangnail became a major catastrophe. A coach's belch was enclosed in quote marks and inscribed on stone.

On the day of the fire, the Rattler practice had drawn four journalists from the print media, two mini-cams from TV stations and three radio reporters armed with oversized tape recorders.

Excited that a new angle had presented itself, the journalists descended on a startled fire department lieutenant.

Darnell Fox, better known as Fat Fox, represented KOLD, which covered the event live. Fat Fox requested that the interview be delayed until KOLD came off a commercial. It was, but only God knows why. This was normally a highly competitive media market.

Then the questions spewed forth. Was the practice field endangered? Could it be arson? Would there be an investigation?

The lieutenant shrugged. "Shucks, 't warn't nuthing. We started it ourselves. Just burning off the dead grass. Easier than bringing in the big mower."

Dan Devine was the Fossils coach for the week. His background made the next game a tasty morsel on which journalists could chew endlessly. Devine had enjoyed remarkable luck against Michigan, which was to host the Rattlers on Saturday.

It was only a minor stretch to suggest Devine had Michigan's number. Devine had won four of five meetings with Michigan. Three of the four wins were last-minute nail-biters. Lengthy recaps of the four wins graced Phoenix newspapers—and made their way through the usual channels to the bulletin boards of both the Rattlers and Wolverines.

In 1959 Devine's Missouri team nicked Michigan, 20–15. A Missouri substitute quarterback, Bob Haas, led the Tigers on an 80-yard drive into wind and rain to the winning TD in the final minute.

The reports of that game in Detroit and Chicago newspapers were effusive, in the grand old style of Grantland Rice. Devine kept the clippings handy. Anytime one of his teams faced a big opponent, Devine resurrected those yellowed clippings, which he considered a silent pep talk.

"I figure those clippings won four or five more games for us over the years," said Devine.

In 1969 Missouri blew Michigan away, 40–17, one of the worst losses suffered by Bo Schembechler.

Michigan won 28–14 over Devine's Notre Dame team in 1978, but the next year Notre Dame beat Michigan, 12–10. Jo Devine, the coach's wife, refused to watch the last play, a field goal attempt which could have won the game for Michigan. But she was the first in her area to jump up and shout, "We win, we win."

She had heard two thumps. The first was the thump of foot hitting football. The second thump, she correctly concluded, came as the attempted field goal was being blocked.

It was blocked by celebrated linebacker Bob Crable, who gained elevation by vaulting off the back of a hunched-over lineman. The move is no longer legal but the Rattlers would devise a latter-day "legal" version of that play.

The 1980 Michigan game, won 29–27 by Notre Dame, has become a part of Irish lore. It is known as "The Day the Wind Stood Still."

Harry Oliver missed an extra point and a field goal for Notre Dame that day but hit a 51-yard field goal at the end to win it. He was kicking into a stout wind, which, according to Irish historians, suddenly subsided briefly for the boot.

The ability to still windstorms apparently was lost when Devine left Notre Dame. At least, the wind did not stand still when his Rattlers invaded Ann Arbor on that mid-November Saturday. Far from it.

The wind blew at 25 to 35 miles per hour, turning temperatures in the 20s into a below-zero chill factor. Stinging sleet peppered pads. Thermal underwear, turtle necks, gloves and sideline space heaters labored unsuccessfully to provide a modicum of comfort. Devine called the safest play possible on the Rattlers first scrimmage attempt. Quarterback Bobby Joe Jackson, his hands warmed by the Kangaroo-type pouch on his jersey, accepted the ball cleanly from the center. He stuck the football into the gut of the onrushing fullback, Bill Bovine, who promptly fumbled.

Bill explained later that his fingers, encased in skin-tight skin-diver gloves, simply would not bend. He said he couldn't decide if the gloves were too tight or his hands too cold.

Either way, Michigan recovered and four plays and 20 yards later had a 7–0 lead.

Devine knew cold. He grew up in Minnesota, was an assistant coach at Michigan State and a head coach in Green Bay, Wisconsin. He was packed into a snowmobile suit. And somewhere from his chilly background emerged an old hunk of foul-weather strategy.

The best play on a frozen field, went the theory, was a pass because the receiver knew where he was going and the defensive player didn't. A short hook pass over the middle was called. End Jones Keith knew where he was going. He just didn't get there. As he whirled on the button-hook, his feet skidded out from under him.

The pass, already underway from Bobby Joe Jackson, sailed over the fallen Keith into the hands of Michigan safety Hans Schroeder. Schroeder sped to the right flank, recently vacated by Keith, and went 27 yards to score. It was 14–0 Michigan with only four minutes gone.

Predictably, Michigan became ultra conservative and Southwestern hesitated to take more chances. So, the Rattlers trailed 14–0 at half-time.

Half-time dressing rooms, unlike public perception of them, usually follow the same routine. Position coaches work with players on minor adjustments after which, the head coach normally delivers his brief, emotional "Go-Get-'em" speech.

Devine was from the old school. He took over the half-time proceedings. First, his puzzled players were served hot chicken soup from a big vat. Then they were told to change from cleated shoes into tennis shoes.

Devine explained how his Packers found footing by changing to sneakers in a division championship game at Minnesota and won. Then he explained the chicken soup, which was a longer, more-emotional story.

"You guys are mentally beat, but you can win this game," Devine said. "Let me tell you about the 1979 Cotton Bowl game. Notre Dame team played against Houston. A sudden cold snap hit Dallas. It surprised all of us, left us shivering, especially, Joe Montana. Our quarterback was not himself. He had thrown three interceptions. At half-time our doctor, Les Bodnar, took his temperature. It was 96. Joe was suffering from hypothermia.

"The doctor was a good one. He came prepared for everything, even that cold snap. He reached down in that black bag of his and pulled out a can of chicken soup. He heated it on a radiator. Joe slurped it up. But when we went out after the half-time break, Joe didn't go. He stayed in the dressing room, sipping more soup, and trying to get his temperature up to normal.

"We were a beaten team when Joe came out at the end of the third period. We're behind, 34–12 with 7:37 remaining. It all turned around with a blocked kick. That led to a Notre Dame touchdown. We added the two-point conversion and it was 34–20.

"Montana steps up then. He hits three straight passes and rolls out for two yards and the touchdown. We get another two pointer.. It's 34–28.

"I really thought we had blown it when Montana fumbled on the Houston 20 after a 16-yard run. Now, there's only two minutes. We use our last two time-outs to stop the clock. Houston has a fourth and one at the Houston 29 and gambles on a run rather than punt. We stop them. Joe throws for a touchdown with two seconds left. We kick the point and win 35–34 in maybe the best comeback I've ever seen.

"The predicament you guys face now isn't nearly as tough as that was. You can win this football game. You are the better team. Believe it and act like it and you will win."

Devine decided to strike while the players were hot. Well sort of hot. The fake punt was a Devine trademark. But this was a fake with a twist— a fake introduced by Joe Kapp when he coached at California.

It was third and ten from the Southwestern 20. Considering the elements, no one was surprised when the Rattlers lined up in deep punt formation on third down. As the play started, Rod Norman went through his full kicking motion. But the ball was not snapped to him. It went to quarterback Bobby Joe Jackson, one of three players lined up short behind the center, ostensibly as blockers. Bobby Joe, hunched low behind the blocker in front of him, then launched a high spiral which was designed to resemble a punt, which it did.

The Michigan returner, Woodson Herring, thought it was a punt. His right arm shot skyward, the signal for a fair catch. Southwestern's two wideouts, Jones Keith and John Ramsey, converged in front of Herring.

Understand, please, that the Rattlers at this point faced a win-win situation on this weird play. They could catch the pass for a completion. Or, they could hope Herring would battle them for the football, in which case Herring would be guilty of pass interference.

Herring was relaxed, thinking he was protected by the fair catch signal. His eye was fastened on the descending football. Ramsey stepped in front of Herring, caught the ball, and took off. Keith blocked Herring. Result: Touchdown. Suddenly, Southwestern was back in the game, trailing only 14–7.

On the next Rattler possession, Devine went for another fake punt. Michigan reasonably thought the last thing it would see was back-to-back fake punts, especially from a conservative coach like Devine. A little research might have made them more wary. Dan's teams had scored three times on fake punts.

This one, Devine explained later, was a replica of one his Irish used against Arizona. It was a true fake in that it faked teammates as well as opponents.

Only two people, the kicker and Devine, knew it was coming. It was to be used only against a 10-man rush.

Devine twirled his whistle. This was the "go" signal. The Rattler kicker, Aussie Rod Norman, was instructed to watch the outside rusher on his right. If he rushed hard to the inside, Norman was to run outside.

It worked for Notre Dame's Blair Kiel years earlier against Arizona. Kiel went 80 yards and a touchdown.

"If it hadn't worked," said Devine, "If it hadn't I'd still be at Notre Dame—hanging from a cross. "

And it worked again for Norman this chilly day in Michigan. The Aussie raced 65 yards to score. Devine, on a roll, then decided to strike again when the iron was hot—or more to the point, while his players were still warm.

This may have been the most gutsy call of all. The Rattlers opted to go for two—and with the scout team which had developed some expertise at running the triple-option offense. But this was the quadruple option. Quarterback Jose Garcia went through the first three options: (1) A fake to the fullback; (2) a fake by the quarterback off tackle; (3) A fake lateral to the trailing halfback.

Then up popped the fourth option in the "Triple Option" offense—a pass to tight end Muhammad Jones.

Garcia and Jones were basketball teammates. This one was out of the basketball play book. It was a chest pass, a lob or alley-oop pass. In basketball, Jones leaped and caught the ball and stuffed it before returning to the floor.

The football version was much the same, except there was no net through which to stuff the ball. Jones only had to return to mother earth with ball in grasp. It mattered not whether Muhammad was covered. He stands 6-foot-8 and had a vertical jump of 38 inches. As he soared into the stratosphere against Michigan, he left defenders clawing ineffectively at his mid-section. So, it was two points and a 15–14 Southwestern lead.

And it stayed that way although it became a tight-wire act for the Rattlers at game's end. Michigan drove to the Southwestern 25-yard line with two seconds left. A 42-yard field goal was a chip shot for Michigan's Tom "The Toe" Trimble.

Clippings of Crable's leap-frog field goal block in 1980 had been on the Michigan bulletin board. Trimble had it on his mind.

But Trimble faced an unexpected, different type problem. The Rattlers had been rehearsing for just such a situation. Muhammad Jones, all 6–8 of him, was stationed in the middle of the Rattler line. At the snap of the football, he started waving and jumping up and down and to and fro, like a puppet on snarled strings.

Jones had set a school record for basketball blocks, and practice sessions produced high hopes for continuation of the feat on the football field.

His crazy jumping jack act did not add to his block total, but it distracted Trimble so badly he shanked his field goal attempt, sealing the Southwestern victory.

CHAPTER 22

One prominent coach has suggested that behind every successful football program is a cooperative university president. That may be exaggerated but now, more than ever, the buck for successful athletics stops at the president's oversized desk.

In a sense, presidents have validated their growing interest in athletics by seizing control of the NCAA from their appointed aides, the faculty representatives.

This overemphasizes athletics' status in the overall scheme of education. Still it is practical. Football makes and spends more money than any other department and is, face it, a public relations tool through which many alums, unfortunately, grade the institution.

The trend, as a result, is that athletic directors communicate directly with the college presidents, rather than report through some vice president.

Southwestern hasn't followed the trend. There, the athletic department business is channeled through a vice president, the same vice president who led the futile search for coaches who could take over in mid-season. His name is Percival N. Pickens.

"Don't call me Percy," he warns those brave enough to do so.

God knows what he would do if told his full, behind-the-back nickname. Which is "Percy Nitpicker."

An exact fit, this, for the sour, puffed-up busybody. Athletic department secretaries claim he drops by every so often to count the paper clips and audit the duplicating machine's output.

Percy is troublesome but not dangerous until he pulls out his copy of the NCAA rulesbook. This publication is so large and so complex that nit-pickers can find a nit to pick on virtually every page.

No item was too small for Percy to blow out of proportion. A case in point was the list of athletic department misdemeanors Percy placed on President Justin White's desk.

Some in the athletic department theorized Percy was seeking revenge for being so ignominiously ousted from the search committee. White had appointed me, Shirley Tate and Percy to find new coaches when Boots and his staff were fired. Percy smelled opportunity knocking. In a grandstand move designed to gain a promotion, he appointed himself as a one-man search committee. He failed miserably. And where he failed, Shirley and I succeeded by luring prominent coaches out of retirement.

With that defeat, Percy retreated into the background. But he was to resurface a month and a half later with a carefully-compiled list of alleged athletic department indiscretions. President White would have liked to torch the list, but felt compelled to call a meeting.

So it was that Percy, Devine, Shirley and I circled the president's desk to hear the charges.

"We all know that the coach can not make any kind of cash payment to a student-athlete," Pickens said, then turned to Devine. "You, sir, should know better. You have been a head coach at three major universities. You had to know this was a violation."

Devine shrugged, shaking his head sadly. "Yes, sir, I did. But the youngster in question, a third-team halfback named Larry Cushman, came to my office on a Sunday morning. His grandmother, who brought him up, had died and the funeral was early the next morning in Los Angeles.

"The kid was broke. He needed 33 bucks to ride a bus to Los Angles. I gave it to him. Yes, I knew it was a violation."

Shirley raised her hand to silence the coach. "The one thing the NCAA exercises occasionally is the law of reason. Dan brought his problem to me. I arranged for Larry to get a student loan for $33 when he returned on Tuesday. He did and he repaid Dan immediately. I immoderately contacted the NCAA official in charge of enforcement, David Price, who understood the problem and approved of the way we handled it."

Dr. White turned to Percy, both hands upturned in a question. "Why all the fuss, Percy?"

Percival started to correct the president on the nickname but thought better of it and went on to item No. 2.

"Yes sir, I think that is a reasonable resolution of a knotty problem. But I have another one that won't be as easily resolved.

"I have it on good authority that the athletic department helped furnish a new apartment for three of its best freshman prospects."

Devine laughed. "Yes sir, Percy," he said, knowing that Percival would not correct him in front of the president. "What you've uncovered here is a real felony. Maybe we all could get life for this.

"You would have to know Joanne Shaffer. She runs our office. There is no way this staff could have managed without her around. Besides looking after the coaches, she considers herself a mother to all the players.

"One day the three players you were talking about were sitting in the football office. The three had rented an apartment and were wondering how to get towels and bed sheets. Joanne interrupted.

"She said, 'I've got some stuff I plan to give to Good Will. You can have it if you want it.'"

Shirley took over. "The incident was reported to me. I looked at the linens. Believe me, they had no value to anyone. Good Will might have turned them down. I filed a written report to the NCAA. Haven't heard from them so I guess its OK."

By now, President White was losing his patience. "If you don't have anything better than this, Percy."

"But I do, sir. One of the best football recruits in the country is James Watts, here in Phoenix. Great running back. The NCAA is watching over his shoulder. They know somebody will cheat to get him. I regret to tell you that we are guilty. A Southwest alum took him out to dinner, a clear violation."

It was Shirley's turn to laugh, as she took over the witness stand from Devine.

"This gentlemen, is becoming ludicrous. The NCAA has already investigated that and exonerated us of any wrong doing. Turns out the alum lives next door to Watts. The families have interrelated since the boy was twelve years old. The two families always have a cookout on Sundays. One week it's the Watts, the next week it's at the alum's. The NCAA just made a common sense decision. Which, I might say, we've seen very little of here, if you'll pardon the dangling preposition, Dr. White."

"Consider yourself pardoned," said White. "What is harder to pardon is why we're all wasting our time here."

"Well, there is one more thing I wanted to bring up," said Percy. "This isn't a violation but I think it undermines what we are trying to do academically. I appreciate the Fossils have done, but I don't appreciate the course they have introduced. They are trying to make this a trade school rather than a reputable four-year university."

Devine had had it. You could see him twitch.

"Mr. President I am probably negligent in not bringing this to your attention earlier."

"There is much talk about exploiting the athlete these days. Frankly, the talk doesn't bother me. At least we are giving these athletes an opportunity for a good education. But we, and I speak of the Fossils, feel we want to do more. We have started a no-credit course on Sunday afternoon. We call is Professional Football 101. It is for those who plan to go into the NFL or coaching. Attendance is voluntary, but the course attracts overflow crowds.

"We try to bring in former players, public relations experts, lawyers, financial advisers, experts on NCAA rules and athletic administration. Most of all, we tell players how to pick agents, how to recognize the good and bad agents. Whether or not the ones attending receive a degree they will, at least, be better prepared to face the life of their choosing."

President White nodded, and then turned on Percy.

"Sir, in my opinion, our part-time coaches are handling these problems in an exemplary fashion. They should be praised not censured."

"And as for you, Mr. Nitpicker, you no longer will be in charge of athletics. The athletic department will report directly to me."

The president was so worked up he did not realize he had used the forbidden last name of Percy.

CHAPTER 23

The Arizona Republic is a rather strange name for a newspaper-a fact brought to my attention when I introduced myself to Darryl Rogers, who became the Arizona State football coach in 1980.

"My name is Bull Bullington," I said. "I'm with The Arizona Republic."

"Aren't we all?" deadpanned Darryl.

Rogers followed Frank Kush as coach at ASU, Well, almost. Kush departed after three games the previous season primarily because, it was alleged, he socked a punter after a poor punt. It was only natural, then, that Rogers was asked if he had ever hit a player.

"No, not even when I was a player," the coach responded.

In retrospect, what stands out in my mind about Rogers was his dry, quick humor. It was not the leg-slapping, manufactured humor many coaches collect for banquet speeches. It was a spontaneous humor drawn easily from what was transpiring around him at the moment.

Once, the bus carrying his ASU team to the University of California Memorial stadium got lost meandering through the Berkeley hills. This renowned hillside campus has spawned some of the greatest thinkers of our time. And the greatest stinkers, too. As a carryover to its hippy days, Cal has its share of unwashed students dressed in scruffy duds.

With the kickoff nearing, a nervous Rogers stepped into the stairwell adjacent to the driver. The bus pulled up at a stop light.

"Would you look at that," said a voice at the rear.

Eyes turned to a ill-kempt, long-haired youngster standing on the corner with a boa constrictor wrapped around his neck.

Darryl looked at the strange sight, turned to the bus driver and said, "Well, we're here. Welcome to the Cal campus."

It is commonly accepted in the sports profession that, when making a coaching change, it is best to make a big change. ASU apparently subscribed to this notion by replacing the short, tense, brash Kush with the tall, loose, laid-back Rogers.

In sharp contrast to Kush's tough practices were the almost casual practices under Rogers. It is said, although not confirmed, that when Rogers was coaching at Fresno State he ran his players through wind sprints by having them retrieve the golf balls he wedged from one endzone to the other.

Rogers had a keen offensive mind. He ran the west coast offense before it was called that. He was a passing disciple of Sid Gillman, who pioneered the possession pass attack.

Rogers featured speed. On the field and off, but especially at the dinner table. He could consume a meal in one big gulp. Or so it seemed. Normal diners would be toying with the salad and he'd be devouring a desert.

Why in such a hurry, some brave soul asked.

Darryl was frank about it. He grew up eating meals as a guest at friends' houses. The faster he ate the more he could consume.

Rogers spent his early years in Long Beach, Calif., house hopping. His parents were divorced when he was 8. Darryl grew unhappy with the situation at home and. as a ninth grader, moved in with a brother. He later lived with families of four different friends.

Young Darryl picked up pocket change working for the Long Beach recreation department. Among those to whom he gave tennis lessons was a seven-year-old named Billie Moffitt, who grew up to be Billie Jean King.

Perhaps, the unsettled youth prepared Rogers in some manner for the adversity he faced in coaching. At both Michigan State and Arizona State, he took over programs that were on NCAA probation. He was 24–18–2 at Michigan State, 37–18–1 at ASU.

When Rogers left ASU after the 1984 season to become the Detroit Lions coach no oversized tears were shed. His won-loss passed muster, but that one tie is what turned off Arizona State fans. Stuck in their collective craw was a 26–26 deadlock with UCLA in 1983.

Seldom has a tie been so blown out of proportion. At least not since the 1966 Notre Dame-Michigan State game when Irish Coach Ara Parseghian allegedly settled for a 10–10 tie.

In that ASU game with UCLA, the Devils jumped to a 26–10 lead over the Uclans, but crumbled in the fourth period. Everything went wrong. Interceptions, key penalties. UCLA scored twice, and made one two-point conversion and missed another. However, the Bruins were given a second chance after the miss because Arizona State was detected holding. The second try was successful.

The collapse might have been forgiven. But not forgivable was what happened when ASU took over on its own 20 with 1:36 left. The Devils went into a shell to protect the tie. Four straight running plays made it obvious they were settling for the deadlock. It's doubtful if any four plays anywhere changed the perception of a coach as much as these did.

Rogers explained a tie rather than a loss in a conference game might end up paving the way to the Rose Bowl. ASU had not tied in 229 straight games. To settle for a tie tore at the innards of the fans.

Rogers was ridiculed and harangued. He was "Fit to Be Tied," said one newspaper. Ties were suggested as an appropriate Christmas present for Rogers. One group of fans entitled their informal golf tournament the "No-Balls Open" to commemorate the deadlock.

An untied Rogers might have lived happily ever after at ASU. Heck, the team he recruited was to win the Rose Bowl the following year under John Cooper.

Despite the full-larder and a good record at ASU, Rogers was ready to go when the Lions came waving a job in his face. After he went 18–40–0 in four seasons, the Lions fired him.

Rogers desperately yearned for another coaching job. It was, he said in retrospect, a matter of timing. That is the pity of coaching. You are hot or you are not. Rogers had been much in demand. When he was hot at San Jose State, he once juggled three job offers at one time. In 1978. when Rogers' Michigan Staters kicked cross-state rivals, Michigan, 24–15 to win a share of the Big Ten title, he again was besieged with new coaching bids. After his ASU teams led the nation in defense in 1981 and in offense in 1982, Rogers again was a target in coaching hunts.

But after being fired by the Lions in 1988, Rogers got nothing but snubs from football head hunters. Which was too bad. The guy was only 53. He loved coaching and was good at it. He loved it so much he eventually took what turned out to be a non-paying job coaching a semipro team in Oklahoma City.

So, Rogers was grateful for the opportunity the Fossils provided to coach another Arizona team. And he wouldn't have to worry about another tie. College football had installed the tie-breaker rule, which made a tie impossible.

Under the new plan, tied teams would keep playing overtimes until a decision was reached. In the college tiebreaker, which the NFL should adopt, each team is given a possession starting 25 yards from the goal. If the score is tied after the two possessions, the teams move on to another overtime.

Darryl had already grown fond of the change. Southern Connecticut State, where he wound up as athletic director, had won two big games with the tiebreaker.

After the second one, Rogers sighed and said, "My how I wish they had that rule when I was coaching. It would have made my life much more simple."

CHAPTER 24

Pullman, home of Washington State University, is isolated in the gently-rolling hills and on the eastern border of Washington. It is 75 miles south of Spokane and 285 miles southeast of Seattle. "It is not the end of the world," said its one-time basketball coach, George Raveling. "But you can see it from there."

Which unfairly demeans Pullman. It is a friendly town of 24,000, 19,700 of whom are students. It emphasizes family values and outdoor sports. Although marooned from civilization, it has claims to fame.

It is named after the man who invented the railroad sleeping car. It is the birthplace of the automatic-leveling combine, which may be found on hilly wheat fields throughout the world. And, it is the self-proclaimed lentil capital of the world. The summer Lentil Festival is the social highlight of the year.

And, Pullman basks in the reflected glory of Washington State football, whose success baffles experts. Football supposedly can not grow and prosper away from large population areas, which serve as the base for athletes and fans.

In theory, the Cougar football program should be a deadend for coaches and players. It is, instead, a stepping stone.

Consider coaches who have moved on to better things: Jackie Sherrill to Pittsburgh, Warren Powers to Missouri, Jim Walden to Iowa State and Dennis Erickson to Miami and then the Seattle Seahawks.

Consider also the quarterbacks spawned at Washington State: Jack Thompson, Mark Rypien, Timm Rosenbach, Drew Bledsoe and Ryan Leaf. NFL teams used first-round picks on all except Rypien.

In a era in which footballers come in two flavors, greedy and grabby, Washington State has produced notable exceptions. Bledsoe, Rypien and Leaf have made substantial contributions, all exceeding $125,000, to endow football scholarships for the Cougars.

November weather in Pullman is consistently inconsistent. Temperatures fluctuate between 20 and 40 degrees, and are more easily tolerated than the rain or sleet or snow which accompany them.

But this particular Saturday in late November was crisp and clear. Snow was banked around the field, but the playing surface itself was dry and fast. The temperature was 40 but bright sunshine made it seem warmer.

Darryl Rogers, the Southwestern coach of the day, and Mike Price, the Washington State coach, met at midfield prior to kickoff. Such meetings are much like baseball's meeting of pitcher and catcher at the mound. Rarely is anything of great importance said.

"How's the family, Darryl?"

"Great, and how's yours?"

"Just fine, thank you."

"Grass looks great. What kind of fertilizer you use, Mike?"

That was a needle. WSU plays on Astroturf.

"Once in a while we put some Woolite on it," deadpanned Price. "That and a vacuum cleaner.

"By the way, Darryl, I understand you are staying over tonight. Wish you and your staff would come by the house after the game for a drink and sandwiches. We can talk over those illegal trick plays you use."

"Sounds great and we'll be there," Darryl said. "But don't think we're going to hold back on any trick plays."

"Wouldn't want you to," Price said. "We've got a few tricks ready for you, too."

Each knew the other was not kidding. Price, like Rogers, was ready to try anything. I mean, who else has coaches and players dressed in tuxedos for their pictures in the press book. When he was at Weber State, Price had a truck loaded with popsicles drive on the field, interrupting practice for a popsicle break.

Success has moderated Price's behavior. Things like popsicle breaks have been mothballed since WSU's trip to the Rose Bowl after the 1997 season. A Rose Bowl coach is expected to exhibit more dignity and respect for the game, Price was told. The coach didn't buy that, but was willing to sacrifice to please his elders-especially those with large wallets.

Price, however, has not outgrown trick plays. He features the flanker. The Cougs run a flanker reverse, and a flanker reverse pass. More staid rivals have asked Price when he plans to quit such things. To which he replies, "When you figure out how to stop them."

The kickoff was at 5 p.m., which cut into supper time in Pullman and robbed the paying fans of at least one half of football in bright sun. Why the late start? The usual reason. Because a television network demanded it.

So what if the kickoff time listed on the tickets was 1:30 p.m. Obligations to customers become secondary to the exposure and bucks of a national TV appearance. It's a pity universities don't unite and stand up to the demands of that one-eyed monster's keepers. The NCAA, bless its sanctimonious soul, takes an unyielding stance on everything except its dealings with television moguls.

So, Southwestern kicked off at 5 p.m. Price had warned his troops that the Rattlers would opt to kick off even if they won the toss. And he was correct. Rogers had opened one of Fresno State's games with an onside kick attempt. Worked well, except for one thing. The kicker whiffed. A human toe never touched football. On the re-kick, the ball was booted deep.

But it was that memory which led to an opening onside kick in the Nebraska game. It led to the only Rattler touchdown. Price was convinced a similar kick would be tried against WSU. He put his "good hands people" on the field. That is, running backs and receivers accustomed to catching the football under pressure.

Furthermore, he instructed his team to watch how the Rattlers lined up for the kickoff.

"If Southwestern puts more players on one side of the kicker than the other, it's a tip-off" Price said, "'You can bet your knee pads the kickoff is going to the side on which they station the most men."

On the opening kickoff, Norman, the Aussie toe, dribbled the ball nicely downfield, a tactic he rehearsed extensively in preparation for the Cougars.

An onside kick must travel 10 yards before the kicking team may legally recover it. But if the receiving team makes the mistake of touching the ball within that first 10-yard no-man's land, either team may recover it, thereby gaining possession.

None of that took into account WSU's swift halfback, Al Marcus. He was pumped up by the opportunity. The picture was unfolding just as the Coach Price said it would. The lineup tipped off an onside kick attempt would be to the right. The kicker kicked short. It hopped high. Marcus didn't wait for the second hop.

He charged the kick. Southwestern players were stunned. Here was some silly guy fielding the onside attempt after it had traveled only seven yards. Dangerous, at best. Foolhardy, in most coaches' books.

The shortened kick was fielded on the first hop chest-high by a speeding Marcus. He simply kept going straight ahead. The Southwestern players were momentarily stunned by the daring maneuver. Never had a kickoff receiving team attacked the onside attempt so aggressively. Not a human hand was laid on Marcus. He was through the first wave of the kicking team before Southwestern players knew it. Never has a kickoff been returned so easily 43 yards for a touchdown. The conversion left WSU ahead 7–0 only 15 seconds into the game.

Within the first three minutes, the lead grew to 14–0. On their next possession, the Cougars again dipped into their bag of tricks.

Price's team used the flanker reverse or the flanker reverse pass on the average of four times a year. The Rattlers had seen the play run and re-run in that week's rehearsal. Rattler defensive ends had been warned to stay at home.

"I don't care where the motion is, or which direction the guards pull, I want you to stay put," Onofrio instructed his ends. "Don't let anybody outside of you, even if he's carrying a bass drum."

So, what happened? The Rattler left end, Rip Replogle, angry at the backfiring onside kick, determined to take his wrath out on WSU quarterback R. J. Commons. The quarterback spun out to his left with Rip in pursuit. Just as Rip laid hands on Commons, the quarterback handed off to flanker back Bill Brownyn headed in the opposite direction toward the area vacated by Replogle.

The Rattler cornerback came up to stop Brownyn. That left wide end J. S. Mashburn wide open. Brownyn lofted a dying-duck-type pass but it was good enough. Mashburn fielded it and ran 10 more yards for a Cougar touchdown.

The twice-outwitted Rattler coaching staff huddled briefly on the sideline. "We have to do something to take the momentum away from them," said Devine. "How about the double cross?" said Rogers.

Two of the coaches gulped. This play was dangerous. It had not been set up properly, by an earlier single reverse, and it took an eternity to run.

The double cross was a double entendre. This basically was a double reverse with a pass. But it also was a double cross because it was a WSU play being used against WSU. The Cougs scored a 49-yard touchdown on it on the first play against California in 1993.

The play was shown to the Rattler defense in practice. It looked so good that the Rattlers decided to add it to their bag of dirty tricks.

Onofrio, perhaps the most conservative of the Fossils, ended the hesitation. "What the heck, men," he said. "This is the last game we'll ever coach. Let it all hang out. Besides, for a trick play to work it has to be the least expected thing you can do."

Sub quarterback Jose Garcia handed to wide receiver Jones Keith going left. Keith then handed to Bobby Joe Jackson going the other direction. Jackson, normally the quarterback, had lined up as a flanker on the left. The defense was temporarily petrified. Their only moving parts were their heads, which swiveled like fans at a tennis match as they looked left, then right. The play took forever.

"A trick play is like sex," once said Pepper Rodgers, a coach at UCLA, Kansas and Georgia Tech. "The longer it takes the better it is."

Quite satisfying to the Rattlers was this toss. The 52-yard missile was fielded by John Ramsey on the 20-yard line. Against no resistance, he went in to score.

Enough tricks? Sure, but the Rattlers still had one in reserve. With no more games to save it for, they unearthed an offering from the trick catalogue of Homer Smith, celebrated as an outstanding offensive coordinator at UCLA, Alabama and Arizona.

Only three minutes remained in the first half. Southwestern tailback Tim Pruitt and wingback Rashad Moshier went in motion at the same time and ran into each other. They argued heatedly, in a helmet-to-helmet confrontation.

The amused defense relaxed, and watched. Pruitt and Moshier made certain they froze motionless for the one second required by the rules. While they held, the ball was snapped. Bobby Joe Jackson lofted a short pass in the vacant flat opposite the argument to Jones Keith. Left flat-footed, the defense had no chance to catch Keith, and he sprinted 67 yards to the tying touchdown. So, it was 14–14 at halftime.

The television people were ecstatic. The trickery opened conversational faucets, and provided record opportunities for meaningful reruns.

Weather had not been a factor in the first half. But after the day in the sleet at Michigan, Southwestern was prepared with soup. It wasn't the chicken soup served at Michigan but lentil soup, served in honor of the area. Who said college football isn't educational?

Changes in strategy were minimal. No pep talks were needed. Coaches felt the Rattlers had Big Mo on their side.

But as the teams moved up the tunnel to the field, a small explosion punctuated the clear, still night. A transformer had blown. Suddenly, fans and field were left in the dark.

Game officials and school officials consulted. It was decided to send teams back to the dressing rooms. Located some 100 yards away from the grandstands, the Southwestern dressing rooms still had electricity.

After 30 minutes in the dark, the referee recalled the head coaches to a midfield conference. The flashlights on three security policemen shed some light on the situation, so to speak.

Why they couldn't meet in the well-lighted warm interior of the dressing area was not explained. Perhaps officials felt fans who paid to see the game should see it end.

And end it did with that summit meeting at midfield.

Referee Tim Sidena patiently explained that all possibilities had been explored. A quick fix was impossible. Portable floodlights were unavailable.

"There's nothing we can do," he said, except to declare the game a tie."

"But you can't have a tie anymore," Rogers protested. "Can't we play it off someway, somehow, somewhere?"

"Sure, we'll have all the people in the stands turn on their Ericsson cell phones and play in the glow they put out," said Price, in reference to a TV commercial.

"No, I'm dead serious about this, Mike." Rogers' voice turned raspy with passion. "If there's anything I don't want it is a tie. I've had one too many ties in my life already."

By now, a television mini-cam had joined the midfield confab. The photographer, with his self-contained power pack, kneeled and aimed his camera and its light up at Rogers

The low-lighting and the anguish on his face made Rogers look like something out of a Frankenstein movie.

"Why not just have a tiebreaker now to decide the winner?" Rogers asked. "We could pull some cars up to the sideline, like we used to do in high school, and play by the headlights."

"Let it go, Darryl," Sidena said. "I know how bad you hate the tie and why. But there's not a damn thing any of us can do about it."

Which was the key.

This was different from the cross Rogers bore for the tie years earlier against UCLA. Then, he decided not to go all out to avoid a tie. Judging from his words and expressions on national TV, Rogers obviously was fighting like hell to prevent a tie against Washington State.

As it was to turn out, Darryl Rogers received public support and public sympathy, not public censure.

CHAPTER 25

The night lights went out in Pullman left Rattler coaches and players limp, unfulfilled and generally down in the dumps. Considering frustration built into the unexpected deadlock, the hangover time was minimal. Most of the disappointment was washed away in warm showers, the rest in the anesthesia of alcohol.

What the hell. No one asked for a tie. No one wanted it. And, this was to become tiny hunk of football history.

It couldn't be allowed to detract from a great season, coaches told players. It had been a season far beyond expectations. For the season, the Rattlers were 9–1–1. They were 6–0–1 since the Fossils took over. A top-ten finish was likely. A bowl bid certainly would have been forthcoming had not Southwestern been barred from post-season play because of the cyberspace scandal.

"A tie is supposed to be like kissing your sister," Devine told players and coaches. "But this one is different. It was not self inflicted. It was imposed by a power failure. So, don't weep over this. Keep your chin up."

Most bought this. Most except Darryl Rogers, who already had one too many ties. Rogers still was despondent as the coaches gathered in Devine's hotel room for a traditional post-game drink. It was a celebration, of sorts, for the others but a wake for Rogers.

Only the coaches and a few friends convened to share the camaraderie of a ceremonial drink. Shirley and I were among the non-coaches invited.

Shirley's acceptance by the coaches was one of the season's more surprising turnarounds. Once she was viewed as a witch and a bitch as the NCAA rules enforcer. She still enforced rules, but Shirley had become an asset. She beefed up the tutoring and study hall facilities. She provided counseling, sometimes even becoming personally involved in helping fringe students be certain they had the best possible class schedules.

Players knew about the post-game drink in Devine's room and on this unusual evening, they wanted to be represented. They sent a delegation of five, led by quarterback Bobby Joe Jackson. He was the obvious spokesman, but the only speaking role was handled, surprisingly, by tackle Michael Matuszak.

Early on, Matuszak had a lot to say about the Fossils, most of it demeaning. Dinosaurs he called the interim coaches. Southwestern, by bringing in over-the-hill coaches, had reduced his chances of playing pro football. It was like Mutuszak was campaigning for a airline ticket out of Phoenix.

But this dissident had gradually altered his opinion until now, at season's end, he was the Fossils' biggest booster among the players. Players followed his lead because he was a leader, a quiet but thoughtful leader.

"I was wrong about you guys," Matuszak told the coaches. "I thought you were a bunch of has beens, old geezers with no idea about football today. I didn't give you much credit. But I was wrong. I learned more football in half a season under you guys that I did in six years under other coaches. So, I'm here to say thanks, not just from me, but for all the other guys on the team.

"And we feel bad that Coach Rogers felt so bad about the tie. So we got him a present."

Linebacker Joe Fridena stuck an oblong box at Rogers. It was borrowed from the trainers. It had once contained rubber gloves. The box was tied with a makeshift bow, formed with a shoe string.

Rogers ripped it off, and opened the box. It did not deserve to see the light of day. A worse tie you never saw. The tie, it later was revealed, was the one tie owned by Fridena. He had never worn it, which was understandable.

The tie was bright green and orange and chartreuse and glowed in the dark. It changed colors as the light changed. It also changed the frown on Rogers face into a smile. This was a tie so bad one could only laugh at it.

So was Fridena's poetry that came with it:

"When problems become more than you can bear
Remember this tie you do not have to wear."

It was a welcome respite, but the coaches still hadn't had their drink. Ice, ordered 30 minutes earlier, had not arrived and the entire group was expected at Mike Price's house in another 30 minutes.

"So what do we do?" asked Mitchell.

"Let me take a shot at it," said Shirley.

We heard only one side of the conversation. But the responses were obvious.

"This is an emergency. Let me talk to the manager on duty." Pause.

"Do you have a doctor in the motel?"

Pause.

"Well is there one on call?"

Pause.

"How long would it take to get him here?"

Pause.

"Well, we've got a man here with a pain in his side. What do we do? Could it be the appendix"

Pause.

"Well, just a minute…our trainer says we need to apply ice to the inflamed area. Get us some ice up here right away."

Shirley put down the phone. Within a minute a bellhop with a big bucket of ice was knocking at the door.

With this performance, Shirley was immediately elevated to honorary coach.

The drinks were gulped. And the glasses were thrown at the fireplace. OK, so the fireplace was fake. So were the plastic glasses. But the symbolic gesture brought closure, to use an already overused term. The tie was behind us.

CHAPTER 26

Mike Price has a nice but unostentatious two-level house on a ridge overlooking the campus. The living area on the upper level is surrounded by a huge deck. Even on this chilly evening, the coaches felt compelled to have at least one beer outside to soak up the view.

Once upon a time, say, four decades ago, such fraternizing among rival coaches was commonplace. Either on a Friday or Saturday night, the home coach would invite his opponents over for a brew.

And the game was better off because of it. Problems were worked out one-on-one rather than before the NCAA council. Rumored under-the-table payments were aired above the table. There were illegal enticements and excessive recruiting visits in those days, as they are now, but coaches were much less likely to cheat on a friendly colleague than on a stranger.

Now, teams fly into town on a chartered aircraft in time for a limbering-up drill on Friday and depart an hour after the game on Saturday. Coaches see one another only at that perfunctory midfield meeting before the game.

So, this was a pleasant throwback to days of yore. Coaches circled Price's fireplace. One by one, they took turns at letting flames lick at still chilled butts.

The usual how's-the-family formalities were traded before Rogers broached a subject uppermost in his troubled mind.

"Mike, what bothers me is how you knew we were going to use that onside kickoff to open the game. Heck, there's no more unlikely time to do that."

Price smiled. He does that easily.

"We just made a good call."

"Who did you call?" Mitchell asked. "Joe Paterno?"

After a brief pause for chuckles, Price continued. "Well, it was a gamble. But there wasn't that much to lose. We've still got three guys back to field deep kicks. We've been looking at your films for two weeks. "

Devine assumed his humble stance, as he does easily. "How do a bunch of over-the-hill coaches rate that kind of attention?"

"Think about it," said Price. "How many times do you run into a team that runs the pro set, the wishbone and the single wing in one game? And think about that other crap you've come up with this year. Throw-back to the quarterback, the old mud-on-the-cleats trick. How many teams show a run-kick option or a draw play that has a five-minute delayed fuse?

"We've got to get ready for a seven-diamond, assorted fake punts, the buck lateral and the old hook and ladder. Or is it hook and lateral? Hell, back in my days we called it a flea flicker. Now they say the flea flicker is when a halfback tosses back to the quarterback who throws a long pass. Hell, even Stephen Spielberg couldn't whomp up a scenario this weird.

"We decided three weeks ago that this was going to be a big game for us. And it was. We got word tonight that the Cotton Bowl is picking us tomorrow. Anyway, three weeks ago, we started preparing for you. Each of our assistants was assigned two of your games to dissect and analyze.

"And then…well, I have this class in sports history. We started a little project this year. Each of our students was told to research a different one of your coaches. And they did a helluva job. They dug up old clippings, reviewed old press guides, and devoured all the Phoenix newspapers.

"I tell you this, you guys ought to be flattered. I doubt if any team anywhere spent so much time trying to get ready. There is no way we could have done it if we hadn't had a week off last week."

Rogers' patience was stretched. "But the onside kick, Mike? What made you so sure we'd try it on the opening kickoff?"

"Well, first we see where you guys open against Nebraska with an onside kick. Then, one of our students brings in a clipping telling how you tried it when you were at Fresno State but the kicker whiffed. Against Cal Poly, I think. Another student double checks an old Fresno brochure. It checked out. So, we felt like it was worth a shot, anyway."

The Fossils looked at one another, heads cocked. Obviously, an idea was building up in their minds. Proving telepathy is not a forgotten art, most of the Fossils nodded their approval to what others were thinking.

This guy Price was impressive. And a pretty good ol' boy, too. This was a classic scouting job with a few unique touches added.

Little wonder that Washington State had tied Southwestern. Only way the Cougs could have been better prepared was to have a copy of the Southwestern play book.

Devine arose and apologized to the host. He asked if the Rattler staff could be excused for a few minutes. The six Fossils convened in the chill of the deck.

"I know what you have in mind," said Kush, "And I agree entirely. Price would be a hell of a pick as the new Southwestern head coach."

Devine nodded. "Yes, that's what I was thinking. When I was interim Athletic Director at Missouri we hired Larry Smith. But Mike Price was high in the running. We interviewed him twice. The guy has good credentials. He has his master's degree from Washington State. He played both quarterback and defensive back at Washington State. And he made all the stops going up the ladder, both as a player and as a coach. He was an assistant for the Cougs, and at Puget South and at Missouri. He was head coach at Weber State. I liked him. I think we should make a run at him. Agreed?"

Yes. Unanimously.

The group returned eagerly to the warmth of the fireplace. Devine's attempt at subtlety was quickly unmasked by Price."

"It's great out there on the deck, Mike," said Devine. "But wouldn't you enjoy the kind of weather we have at Phoenix?"

Price chuckled. "You offering me a job Dan?"

"Yes, that's right," said Devine. "Our president told us we would be the screening committee and that we would have to approve any appointment. We talked outside. We feel like you're the man. We'd have to talk to the officials but I'm certain we can give you a better contract."

"God, how flattering."

Devine interrupted. "Hell, we're not trying to snow you. We just think you're the one for the job. And if we had any reputation left we'd stake it on you."

"I can't think of many jobs any better," Price said. "Phoenix would be a great place. You have there what I'll never have here. You have the kind of weather that attracts athletes. You have the population to get big crowds. . and a lot of players to choose from."

"There will be a brief pause here while we all go call our real estate friends," Rogers said.

"Not yet," said Price. "I want to think about it. I'd never make a decision like this when we have another game to play. Going to the Cotton Bowl means a lot to our kids. I have to tell you I feel a great deal of gratitude to Washington State University."

Understandable. WSU gave Mike Price a chance to play major college football. Then it gave him the head coaching job, even though his record at Weber State was only average.

And it kept him through thick and thin. Mainly thin. In his first three years as Washington State's coach, Price heard the wolves howling. His teams won only 13 of their first 33 games. The school didn't desert him. Now he had to determine if he would desert the school.

The Fossils knew what the answer would be but were proud they could make the offer to a person like this.

CHAPTER 27

WSU's trip to the Cotton bowl turned out to be a trip back to the Rose Bowl. The party was breaking up. Onofrio and Mitchell had topcoats on and the others were starting to bundle up when the telephone call came.

"Stop pulling my leg," Price told the telephone. "You can't be serious."

But the reporter calling was serious. In a night game, UCLA, in the throes of one of its worst seasons ever, rose up to beat the University of Southern California, 17–14. It had seemed such a longshot no one seriously considered the possibility.

UCLA had won only three games. USC had won all seven of its conference games and stood at 9–1 overall. The Trojans were ranked No. 6 in the nation and were a 14-point favorite. But UCLA kicked a 49-yard field goal with three seconds left to win it.

The upset no one expected left Southern Cal and Washington State tied in conference play at 7–1. Which team went to the Rose Bowl?

In the case of ties, the Pacific 10 Conference picks its Rose Bowl representative methodically. There are a series of tiebreakers. If one does not dissolve the tie, the teams step onto the next one. The tiebreakers:

One: Best conference record. Both teams were 7–1.

Two: Winner of head-to-head meeting. WSU and USC did not meet this season.

Three: Team with best overall record. USC was 9–2. WSU was 9–1–1. WSU goes to the Rose Bowl.

And if both teams have the same overall record? Rogers knew the answer, a fact which did not keep him from asking it:

"What happens if the Cougars don't tie with us but lose? Who goes then?"

"Well, in that case, we tie USC with a 9–2 overall record," Price said. "After that, the next tiebreaker eliminates the team that played most recently in the Rose Bowl. That would have put USC in the bowl because we went most recently."

The grin widened on Rogers' face. "So sometimes in a conference race, a tie is as good as a win. Funny. They laughed at me when I said the same thing."

CHAPTER 28

This season, the season of the Football Fossils, had a life of its own. It refused to end. Or so it seemed. Coaches, thinking the season ended with a deadlock in the eastern Washington wastelands, were performing the last rites-the bitter-sweet chore of cleaning out their desks.

It's a slow job, largely because each item to be packed evokes a memory. Nostalgia is wrapped up in each letter, picture or memento reviewed.

Most of the memories dredged up are happy ones. Coaches rarely save unhappy ones.

Kush had a bundle of letters, encircled by a rubber band, which praised his coaching in the win over Arizona. Most commented, in one way or another, that ASU had to be stupid to let him get away.

Chuck Fairbanks had not one but two footballs from the Texas game. One was inscribed, "Southwestern 49" and the second one, "Texas 45." An attached note from the players explained that the score was too large to get on one football.

Al Onofrio carefully placed his favorite letter in a brief case. It was from Antonio Fridena, father of linebacker Joe Fridena.

It stated simply, "We want to thank you for your coaching. Our Joe was a rebel. He's still a rebel but you gave him a cause. His life has gained purpose. He's really buckled down to schoolwork. We are grateful." Jack

Mitchell had saved an autographed picture from Jose Garcia, the basketball player he had turned into a wishbone quarterback. The note from Garcia read, "Never thought I would enjoy football as much as basketball. But I did. And I'll never see a quarterback run the option without thinking of it as a two-on-one fastbreak opportunity."

Darryl Rogers had that God-awful tie, which he could fully appreciate now that he had come to terms with the tie on the playing field.

Devine saved for his scrapbook a note from the basketball coach complimenting him for "Getting more out of Muhammad Jones than I ever could."

Coaching, the second time around, had been a revitalizing experience. One of the Fossils (name withheld by request) said nothing, not even Viagra, had done as much to make him feel young as did the return for six games to coaching.

It was with deep regrets but pleasant memories that the coaches packed up. This was the sweet sorrow that Shakespeare wrote about.

Sweet were the memories and the players who made them. Sorrowful was the fact their coaching careers were ending- for a second time.

They would have preferred an extended season.

And derned if that isn't what they got.

The call came from the president's office. Please come immediately, all the coaches were told, to Dr. Justin White's office.

The visit was not unexpected. The coaches had been told they would receive certificates of appreciation from the president and perhaps watches. Watches. What a great present for a retiree. When time no longer is of importance, they gave you a watch.

It was a motley crew that descended on the president's mahogany-paneled office. Kush and Fairbanks wore gym shorts and sneakers. They had a handball game at noon. Mitchell was lost in an oversized warmup suit. Devine had on short Bermuda shorts. Exposed beneath the shorts was his flowered boxer underwear.

Onofrio was the best dressed of all, in a blue plaid shirt with pants to match. He was headed for the links. President White dispensed with the usual pleasantries. "I just got a call from the Citrus Bowl in Orlando. They want us down there to play in their bowl."

Devine interrupted. "But you don't understand, sir. We have been suspended."

"Yes, I know that," said the president. "The bowl people down there feel certain they can get the NCAA to make an exception to our bowl ban because this is for charity. They plan to donate all the proceeds to programs for the elderly.

"Disney is behind the bowl, with money and no little muscle. Disney wants to do something for the senior citizens. And it wants to do something for the Citrus Bowl which annually attracts thousands of people who also visit Disney World.

"So Disney will put $4 million into the bowl, plus sponsor the CBS-TV show.

"The details haven't been worked out. But this bowl will be a bowl for the ages-and a bowl for the aged. Sound corny? Maybe, that's what the Citrus people are planning to call it.

"Everything will be keyed toward the senior citizen. They want to set up a foundation to fund research on diseases of aging, like, say, Alzheimers. The foundation may also subsidize extended care facilities and provide help for those who slip through the cracks in the health care system.

"And that's where the Fossils come in. You guys are the perfect fit for the bowl's new salute-to-seniors format-the world's oldest football staff.

"Whether you've noticed or not, you coaches have become senior citizen icons, heroes to many of the older fans. You've given them hope. If you can be useful at an advanced age, maybe they can be too."

The Fossils' eyes first rolled. Then they stared at each other. The idea was good. The chance of it ever coming to pass was remote. Indeed, the coaches wondered if Dr. White should be fitted for a straitjacket.

"Sorry, mister president, but I can't imagine the NCAA going along with this," said Devine. "Besides, who would play against us?"

Dr. White's face broke into a grin. He was prepared for the question.

"It would be another school with a lot of retirees in the area, and another school which could benefit from a Disney affiliation. It would be the University of Southern California."

The Fossils gulped. Their eyes met, then quickly darted away in a team-like double take. A major Bowl, national TV, USC. Sounded too good to be true.

"Begging your pardon, sir, but Southern Cal will be going to the Cotton bowl," said Kush.

"I know that's what everyone presumed," said Dr. White. "The Cotton bowl had committed to Washington State, but they felt they had to have a fallback position if WSU could not come. So they had an under-the-table deal with Notre Dame to come if Washington State couldn't. That left USC without a major bowl bid, even though it was rated sixth nationally last week. With Southern Cal and Southwestern, the Citrus folks feel they will have two teams at least in the top 15."

Dr. White was so consumed with the idea that he skipped merrily past the No.1. roadblock, that is, getting an NCAA exception to allow Southwestern to participate in a bowl while on probation. The fact was pointed out to him politely.

"But the Citrus people are ready to address that problem," countered the president. "They have contacted a lawyer who has appeared before the NCAA several times and has, indeed, represented the NCAA in litigation. This gentleman, Meyers Donaldson, fortunately lives right here in Phoenix and feels he can get NCAA approval. He has agreed to represent us and the Citrus Bowl has agreed to pick up his tab.

"So, I say let's make the attempt. We don't have anything to lose and a tremendous amount of prestige to gain."

CHAPTER 29

By a few admiring members of the press, Meyers Donaldson was privately known as "the smartest man in the world." That obviously was an exaggeration but not much of one.

As a chairman of the Fiesta Bowl selection committee, Donaldson was a world-class wheeler-dealer, an attribute which frequently led to attracting good teams to the Bowl. His finagling also served the bowl well in negotiating with TV networks or the NCAA.

With Donaldson and others like him, the Fiesta Bowl has progressed from an insignificant postseason event, created primarily for the use of Arizona State, to a bowl capable of regularly staging collegiate football championships.

Donaldson was not an intimidator, yet it was clear he was not intimidated at all by the solemn and smug souls who rule with evangelistic fervor over the NCAA.

The point is this: He did not come to the NCAA with hat in hand and head respectfully bowed. Indeed, he came in an attack mode.

A mode he also had adopted when the NCAA threatened to block the Fiesta Bowl's move to New Year's Day some years ago. Donaldson countered the NCAA threat to stymie the date change with a hint that such action would prompt an anti-trust suit. The NCAA approved the date change.

Donaldson had some experience in asking the NCAA to lift probation to permit a team to play in a bowl. He approached the NCAA years earlier to inquire if Miami, then banned from bowls, could be given an exception to play "for charity" in the Fiesta Bowl. He felt he was close to convincing the NCAA. Of course, he always feels he is close in a negotiation. But the matter was dropped when Miami lost its last game.

Donaldson once considered running for governor of Arizona. He leaked the possibility to media friends. Trial balloons were launched. Trial failed. Those in and around the Fiesta Bowl would have voted for him but he did not have enough state-wide support.

Meyers developed into an expert at leaking news. He was that person identified in news stories as a "usually reliable source." And he used the technique in launching his campaign for Southwestern.

He first leaked to friends in the Arizona and Florida media that Southwestern and/or the Citrus Bowl would ask the NCAA for an exception to the bowl ban for Southwestern. An open hearing was important, a "usually reliable source" told the media, because an important charity was to receive the proceeds.

Opening closed doors is a popular pastime of newspapers in these times. The NCAA remained in the closet on its Southwestern hearing. But it did consider an unprecedented open meeting, an indicator the august college ruling body was beginning to feel the heat.

The "usually reliable source" also hinted that the NCAA might expect an anti-trust investigation again if it did not at least grant Southwestern a hearing. Senators from Arizona and Florida, encouraged by Donaldson and Citrus Bowl executive Roe Charleston, picked up this issue and carried it to the soapbox.

The NCAA gets a lot of pressure from outsiders. With reason. It has too many rules, many of which are of the nit-picking variety. Yet, if there was not an NCAA, there would have to be something like it. Intercollegiate athletics cries out for a regulatory body. It has become big business. The schools' big-money boosters demand success, which in turn promotes breaking rules.

The NCAA leaders, however, need a course in public relations. They do little to humanize themselves. They normally wear preppy suits and smug smiles, a trend which steamrollered when college presidents assumed control a few years ago. They exude confidence, implying there is no way they could be wrong on any issue.

But the NCAA Board of Directors, all college presidents, were shaken out of well-polished shoes in 1998 by the ruling of a federal judge. He found that the NCAA unlawfully acted in restraint of trade in restricting salaries for the lowest echelon of assistant football coaches. And the supreme court, shrugged off an NCAA appeal on the ruling "without comment."

The anti-trust suit resulted in a $22 million penalty against the NCAA, which by law is trebled to $66 million. A vulnerability suddenly was exposed. NCAA officials spoke with less assurance, if at all. Those who did speak, did so with the promise of anonymity.

Said one: "It is a competitive pressure among us that requires regulations regarding the student-athletes. Now, our greatest concern is that the regulating power could be destroyed or severely limited. I feel there is question whether the NCAA can continue to operate in the same way it has in the past."

Indeed. In addition to the restricted earnings ruling, the NCAA was under fire for standardized tests, allegedly unfair to minorities. A federal judge in Philadelphia threw out the NCAA rule that determines freshman eligibility, declaring it discriminated against African Americans.

Waiting in the wings at the handicapped students, who also claim they are subject to NCAA discrimination.

Meanwhile, congress was starting to question whether presidents, who had assumed control of athletics, were actually in control of their own athletic departments.

Never before had the NCAA rested so uneasily on its throne.

This atmosphere of dwindling NCAA power prompted Donaldson and Charleston to lobby their senators, who as dutiful public servants, took the issue to the senate floor.

"The NCAA has overstepped its vast powers," said Arizona senator Joseph Murphy. "If it is unlawful to regulate the earnings of assistant coaches, it may also be unlawful to control the number of assistants a school may have. Or, limit the number of games it may play.

"Or, establish entrance criteria which may mitigate against minorities. That would greatly reduce their chance of participating in professional sports. Students with learning disabilities could contend they are being deprived of civil rights."

As if on cue, as he actually was, Florida senator X.J. Smith took a more positive approach. "Gentlemen, whether we approve or not, we all recognize intercollegiate sports needs to be able to regulate itself. We need a serious study. Should we consider a commissioner of sports? Or should we give intercollegiate sports a limited exemption to the anti-trust laws, such as baseball now has?"

About this time, a "usually reliable source" reported the Internal Revenue Service was looking into the write-offs claimed by big corporations on blocs of college football tickets.

Donaldson smiled his devious smile in the background.

The NCAA, supposedly immune to pressure, decided to hear the Southwestern request. Southwestern had applied directly to the college presidents who now run the NCAA, not the council that had delivered the decisions in the past. Presidents often are more aware of public feelings, especially the feeling of well-heeled supporters.

The press hopped on the bandwagon. The media dotes on an underdog. There was something appealing about an upstart like Southwestern opposing such formidable opponents as the NCAA and Southern California.

So it was that Donaldson presented himself before the college presidents seated around an elongated and shining walnut conference table in the NCAA's headquarters in suburban Kansas City. It was unprecedented. Also present were the infractions committee and the infractions appeals committee, who first must pass on penalties under the established procedures.

Donaldson did not come with hat in hand as had so many others in confronting NCAA moguls. But that was not to be apparent immediately. Donaldson's dark blue suit was rumpled. So was his hair. He didn't need Rogaine but could have used Head and Shoulders. And the hesitant and apologetic way he opened indicated he also could use public speaking lessons.

"Gentlemen," he said, "I realize that this is...well, what's the word, an imposition. We wouldn't bother you except...well, we feel this is an unusual situation which deserves some...er, ah special consideration."

Dr. Jackson Curtis of Georgia Tech, president of the presidents, shrugged his shoulders impatiently. "Please, sir, would you get to the point. We all are busy men with other items on our agenda."

"Yes sir, yes sir. Beg your pardon. The point is this. The penalty you have invoked on Southwestern, or in reality the one Southwestern invoked on itself, has achieved its desired result.

"Southwestern State dismissed the two students involved in the scandal and all the coaches. So, all the people involved in the infraction are gone. You are only penalizing the innocent, now."

James W. Trimble of Texas interrupted. "Suh, you'all should read our handbook. We are not punishing the individual. We are punishing the university."

"That being the case, suh, I would like to point out what the university has done as a result of your ruling," said Donaldson. "A self-evaluation program, as you recommend, has been established and has resulted in replacing two coaches in other sports.

"New academic counselors and study halls have been added to benefit our student-athletes. It is with some pleasure, suh, that I report the overall improvement in grade-point average among athletes, pardon, make that student athletes. Anyway, the average went up from 2.0 to 2.9 during the first quarter. Projections indicate 57 percent of our student-athletes now are on course to graduate in five years. That's up from 34 percent. We are proud of our academic advances, and see that as strong evidence Southwestern has taken to heart your reprimand. Copies of supporting documents are placed before you.

"I also should remind you that Southwestern first penalized itself with the one-year bowl ban. The NCAA had only to approve the action.

"Procedures now are in place for those who run into trouble off campus. We have had only two such infractions. Those two athletes are on probation, and will be dismissed with another infraction.

"A screening committee will analyze the source of every athletic dona-
tion exceeding $100. Every off-season job for student-athletes will be
scrutinized by the same committee.

"The critical point, gentlemen, is that the penalty you assessed has produced the desired result. By granting an exception, you would be reward-
ing quick and effective action. A reward, I humbly suggest, can be more
effective than a penalty.

"And the reality of the situation is that Southwestern is a new and relatively poor school. A bowl game would be a Godsend, not just for the
money it directly produces but in the ability to solicit donations, enlarge
fan support and improve scheduling."

Barry Robertson of Harvard was the first to arise to speak. His voice
resonated with authority. That, and scholarly assurance.

"You seem unduly concerned with the financial aspect of athletics,"
said he. "We, in this body, are concerned with academics and the general
welfare of the student-athlete. We are not concerned with the finances."

"Oh, is that so?" Donaldson deadpanned. "I'm sorry sir. Since you are
unconcerned with finances, may I suggest that you give away tickets to the
Final Four to students of the competing teams and give away television
rights to Public Television.

"The almighty buck may not be so almighty to the NCAA but I did
notice the courts found you guilty of price fixing salaries of restricted-
earnings coaches. What was the fine, sir? If memory serves it was a pid-
dling $66 million.

"And, one would assume the sweetheart deal that is causing the NCAA
to move its headquarters to Indianapolis may be rooted in finances. "I
would suggest, President Robertson, that you re-examine rules passed by
the NCAA in the past decade. I suggest you would find 75 per cent of
them resulted in cutting costs for athletic departments. Which leads me to
wonder if your organization, like the school I represent, does indeed factor
finances into its decisions."

The Harvard president wasn't at a loss for words. He had a lot of them.
But he couldn't get them out.

"You, you…you're twisting facts. Certainly…the reality is the National Collegiate Athletic Association needs money to operate."

Donaldson interrupted, "And the reality of Southwestern, sir, is that it needs money to operate. We are new. We don't have rich alums. Our students couldn't afford to pay big fees. Our football program must pay its own way, and help subsidize other sports."

"But at Harvard," Dr. Robertson began.

"Begging your pardon, sir, but may I complete this thought," said Donaldson. "Southwestern is much farther away from Harvard than the miles separating the schools. As I was saying, Southwestern is in no way affluent. But Southwestern is prepared to donate all its proceeds from the bowl, above expenses, to charity."

"And what is this charity?" asked Clark Richardson, Stanford, with a chuckle at the line he was about to deliver. "An old-age home for lawyers and retired professors?"

Said Donaldson, "I'm glad you brought that up. The Valley of the Sun, that area encompassing Phoenix and suburbs, has many senior citizens. We propose to address the needs of these people in a direct way.

"Gentlemen, we know you are busy men. We have only one witness. Would someone ask Mrs. Shelly Stewart to come in?"

Entering was a lady who would have to stretch to be five-feet tall. She was stocky. Her hair was thinning on top. Her cheeks were rosy. So was her outlook on life.

"Gentlemen, I'm here to tell you about Meals on Wheels," she said. "That's what we used to call it, anyway. Now it's Home Delivery Service for seniors. We deliver hot meals five days a week to those who are too old, too poor or too infirm to get hot meals for themselves.

"Without this service, these people…well these people would go hungry. People can do without a lot of things but food is not one of them.

"All these recipients must be approved by a case worker. You see all kinds. We have ladies now that are 99 and 102. The food is the one essential but some of the people look forward more to the five-minute conversation with folks that bring the food. We see people every day sitting in the same chair in the same clothes. We see deceased people, too. We call 911 and wait for the paramedics.

"The Salvation Army runs the service I'm with. We serve 88 meals a day in the inner city. The biggest provider is the city. It serves 800 to 1000 meals daily. They are funded with government money."

The president from Texas interrupted. "If the government funds it, why do you need donations?"

"Well, in our case we sure could use a van to replace that 1990 Dodge. It has more than 100,000 miles on it. And as for the city? Well, on their waiting list always are 70 to 100 people who have been pre-approved.

"We can always use donations. We have a deep well. We can soak up everything we get."

"Thank you, Mrs. Stewart," said Donaldson. "I think you all see the need and value of the charity we propose to help.

"We estimate we will be able to donate $1 million from bowl proceeds. The Disney company has volunteered to match anything we can give. A $2 million windfall would provide a deep well."

The presidents looked at each other. Some shrugged. Some nodded heads in approval. Worthy charity. Needy people. Self-imposed ban. Improved safeguards. This would be tough to turn down.

Dr. Jackson Curtis hedged. "We will take this under advisement and get back to you within three days."

It would be touch and go. At least, it would have been had not some "usually reliable source" leaked to the national press the complete details of the meeting. Indeed, every word was quoted accurately, as if someone sneaked a tape recording into the meeting.

Someone did.

The NCAA granted the exception three days later. The game was on.

CHAPTER 30

As bowl week started in Orlando, the Rattler wives were given presents by their husbands–large Waterford salad bowls. Engraved discretely on the bottom of the crystal was simply: "Thanks, from the Fossils."

The second coaching coming of the Fossils had left them with new appreciation for spouses, the unsung heroines in the football world. You hear about the 16 to 18-hour days logged by the coaches but not of the 24-hour stints of their wives as surrogate fathers. In the absence of husbands, the wives become plumbers, electricians, lawn-mowers, chauffeurs, chefs, hostesses, social secretaries and psychologists.

The football wife must cope with husbands' irregular hours and inflated egos. They must muster a smile for obnoxious alums and ignore snubs from snobbish faculty members.

So, the Fossils dedicated their final game of coaching to their wives.

One problem: Dedications have become hackneyed, meaningless gestures. Players and coaches alike were turned on when Knute Rockne implored his Notre Dame team to "Win one for the Gipper."

Nowadays, the Miami Dolphins joke about "winning one for the Flipper."

Today, victories are dedicated to everything from the ball boy's pimple to the coach's ailing second cousin. Most of these dedications are made public only after victories. One wonders how many dedications are conveniently forgotten after defeats.

So, the Fossils, bless them, vowed not to go public with their dedication. Players were to be told of the dedication only before the game, and were to be sworn to secrecy.

The question of the week was this: Which of the six Southwestern coaches would be appointed the head coach for the bowl. It wasn't the serious factor the press made of it. By this point, each of the six coaches had fallen into a comfortable niche. Duties were well defined.

Coaching by committee had not worked for the Chicago Cubs but it did work for the Rattlers. There were no power struggles. This was the end of the coaching line for all of them. None needed a power platform from which to launch further steps up the coaching ladder.

So, who became the head coach for the bowl made little difference. Darryl Rogers had experience against USC. His ASU teams were 2–2 against the Trojans and the 17–10 victory in 1982 was one which had a special place in Rogers' memory bank.

Rogers shook his head in recollection. "One of the finest games I was ever involved in. At Sun Devil stadium. Great crowd. It was just a flat-out good, hard-hitting football game. There's something about Sun Devil stadium in certain instances. I assume every stadium has that for certain games. But our crowd just came alive for that one."

Frank Kush's Sun Devils met Southern Cal only once, but that game was a landmark in ASU football history.

Kush was not particularly happy about ASU moving from the Western Athletic Conference into the Pacific 10 Conference. And his first official Pac Ten game in 1978 reinforced his thoughts as the Devils lost at Washington State, 51–26.

Three weeks later, ASU ran into an even larger roadblock in its home Pac 10 opener against a Southern Cal team ranked No. 1 nationally. Intensely competitive, Kush vowed privately not to be embarrassed again in the Pac Ten. His Sun Devils upset USC, 20–7.

"A great one," said Kush. "I think 12 players from their team made it in the NFL and we had 7 or 8 who did."

So, who did the Rattlers staff elect as their head coach for the bowl? A coach whose teams were 1–5 against the Trojans, Dan Devine.

Actually the coaches didn't vote for Devine as much as for Devine's wife, Jo. Remember, this was a game dedicated privately to wives. Jo Devine epitomized the best in football wives.

Jo Devine was an athlete. In addition to bearing Dan seven children, she found time to win the women's city golf championship of Columbia, Mo.

She was stout but sweet. She has been known to turn to a heckler in the crowd and say, politely, "You are talking about my husband, sir."

Grandstand critics melted under her smile.

As a young woman, she was a true beauty. As an older woman, she showed beauty of another kind. Multiple sclerosis left her with a bowed back and furrowed forehead and confined to a wheel chair. Never has she complained or uttered a cross word to anyone. The smile appeared readily even though she obviously was in pain. Other coaches recognized her game battle with the illness.

Devine's post-Notre Dame speaking tour included a stop at Alabama, where Coach Paul "Bear" Bryant stopped a practice for Jo. She was then able to move about well enough to climb with Bear onto his coaching tower. Ever the southern gentleman, the coach proudly introduced her to his players.

Darryl Rogers, while at Arizona State, professed amazement at one of Jo's feats. "Can you imagine anyone in this day and age raising seven children without an automatic dryer?"

Jo smiled at that. It was her choice. She preferred the smell of clothes hung on an outside clothesline, she said.

Dan denies that Jo, as rumored, frequently shined his shoes.

Jo said it happened. She was Dan's shoeshine girl.

Really? On a regular basis?

"Yes," she said. "Regularly."

Jo Devine never held a regular job. Raising seven kids without a dryer was all one could handle. Nonetheless, Jo was a good provider.

At an NFL meeting in Miami Beach, Jo checked out the buffet table at a conference reception. She gazed at all the goodies and was reminded she had six hungry youngsters back in their room–three from the Devine clan and three more belonging to Hank Stram, Kansas City Chief coach, and his wife.

Jo scooped up mini sandwiches, cakes and assorted tidbits and rolled them up in a napkin. The bulging napkin then was hidden beneath her fur jacket.

As the Devines departed, they ran into NFL commissioner Pete Rozelle and his new bride. Carrie Rozelle extended her hand in friendship. Jo reached out to take it and the jacket opened, allowing the rolled up napkin to drop out. A fancy rug was littered with some of the fanciest hors d'oeuvres in Miami.

Jo can't remember the words that followed. "I guess I blocked them out of my mind, but they both were very understanding."

Yep, and the six kids were still very hungry.

The respect with which Jo was held by other coaches was illustrated by this story: After a football loss, John Robinson stopped the Southern Cal team bus in downtown Tempe, Az, at the sight of a friend. He hopped out, and crossed the street to give Jo a big hug. Ignored was the traffic piling up behind the bus.

Which was ironic, considering that USC was the only team about which Jo Devine ever complained–complaints that seem so out of character for this sweet lady.

She shudders at the mention of the USC Trojans. Looking back on Dan's days at Notre Dame, she said, "I don't think the officials were fair with us when we played them. How do I say it? I think we got rooked."

Devine's Notre Dame team had some close but weird games with USC, which won all but one of their six games against Devine teams. In 1975, the underdog Irish kicked the go-ahead field goal against USC late in the game. The Trojans then mounted a long drive in which the tailback carried 14 straight times. On the 15th play, Quarterback Vince Evans faked to the tailback and ran in for a 24–17 victory.

After USC won again in 1976, by a score of 17–13, Devine was shaking in the dressing room, according to press reports. "I would like to comment on the officiating but I don't believe I should. It's one of the hardest things I've ever done to hold my feelings in."

Devine apparently was referring to two pass interference calls against his standout strong safety, Luther Bradley. One led to a USC touchdown, and the other negated a key Irish interception.

The 1977 game became famous in Irish lore as the "Green Jersey Game." Devine secretly ordered green jerseys, a color worn by Irish in early-day games. He thought it a bit corny but asked his captains for a second opinion. The idea intrigued them: Leprechauns in pads. The green jerseys were waiting in each locker as the team returned from its pre-game workout. Notre Dame won, 49–19.

Notre Dame's Joe Montana, the king of comebacks, staged his all-time best rescue mission in the 1979 Cotton Bowl when he guided the Irish to 23 points in the last 7:37 to beat Houston, 35–34.

Lost in the legends is the fact that Montana engineered nearly as good a comeback in the game preceding the Cotton Bowl, the final regular-season contest of 1978 at Southern Cal. Montana led the Irish on three touchdown drives in the last 10 minutes to take a 25–24 lead. But back came the Trojans with a 37-yard field goal to win.

The march to the field goal was highlighted when USC's Paul McDonald retreated to pass. The ball slipped out of his hands on a pass attempt and the Irish recovered. But was it a fumble or an incomplete pass? The referee ruled for an incomplete pass, a call the Irish faithful still dispute.

Jo Devine had an omen of what was to come, she claims. She was transported to the game that day in a stretch limo furnished by an Irish alum. Jo stepped out of the limo up to her shoe tops into a sizable chunk of horse dung.

Jo is a reasonable person. This hardly seems reasonable but she still thinks that dung was left by Traveler, the white horse which is the Trojan mascot. The horse is ridden by a Trojan warrior, who wears chest armor and a peaked helmet Riddell never made.

Traveler and Warrior circle the Memorial Coliseum field each time USC scores. Jo was tired of that horse running in circles, at Notre Dame's expense. She vowed never to return to that field again. And she has not. But she would be present in Orlando, still carrying a grudge.

CHAPTER 31

Social event of the Citrus Bowl week was the annual luncheon, attended by both teams and most of Orlando's big cigars, and held on the day before the game. It was sponsored by Fixodent. Yep, Fixodent.

The menu was designed either to demonstrate the staying power of the denture adhesive, or to call attention to the need for same. Included was corn on the cob, a rather chewy steak and a desert of candied apples.

Miniature tubes of Fixodent were placed adjacent to each plate along with a sample of Metamucil, a bottle of Centrum Silver and a packet of Dr. Scholl's corn plasters.

Rather unusual favors, these, for the $50 dollar a plate luncheon, but, the table gifts were a tangible reminder of the underlying theme of the game. This was a game for the ages, or aged, if you prefer.

How appropriate. Over 20 percent of Arizona's population is over 65, and that will double by 2020. Only states with more retirees are Florida and California. It was as if this charity game for the elders was booked by the AARP.

The token table medications, designed to stave off the ravages of growing older, should not have been a culture shock for the six Fossils themselves. Remember, they virtually were dragged out of retirement to rescue a coachless Southwestern State team five games into the season. And they immediately had become the darlings of the Geritol-for-lunch bunch. But with each upset and step up the ratings ladder, they had added supporters. The general acceptance and adulation in Arizona tended to obscure where they had come from.

Here, at the Citrus Bowl, they were returned to their roots. They were playing to and for the old folks who popularized them in the first place. They were, to steal an old Darrell Royal line, dancing with the gal that brung them. Their age was what set them apart from other successful staffs, and played a huge role in getting an NCAA pardon.

The unprecedented NCAA reprieve could be traced to the fact that the bowl would benefit worthy senior-citizen enterprises. Remember? The Rattlers would donate profits to a Meals-on-Wheels program. The bowl would donate profits to a foundation for aiding the aged. Disney would match funds.

So, promoters could be excused for milking the senior-citizen angle for all it was worth. There was a movement in central Florida to invite Lawrence Welk and his marching band to perform at half-time, only to find the band didn't march. That uh-one, uh-two, uh-three was not a sergeant's marching cadence, they discovered. Nearest to a march was a couple of overaged tap dancers.

Jules Anderson, president of United Television Company, announced that his sports department, caught up in senior spirit, had arranged a special award for the game's "Most Dependable Performer." Sponsor of the award would be Depends. The two-foot high trophy would be presented by Depends' spokeswoman, June Allyson.

Shirley Jones, Florence Henderson and Betty White, representing other senior-citizen products, were introduced as honorary pompon girls.

Announcement of the "Most Dependable" award prompted a series of titters from the round press table, located in the far right corner of the banquet hall. It accommodated a dozen media freeloaders, most of whom would put the freebie down as a $50 meal on expense accounts.

Scoop Simon started the tittering by suggesting another possible made-for-TV award. "How about one for Feat of the Game, sponsored by Dr. Scholl's."

The Tucson Citizen proposed a trophy for Biggest Hit of Game. "The sponsor could be Ben Gay."

"Or," amended the Tempe Tribune, "Preparation H, depending on which was more appropriate for the area in which the hit was delivered."

The lines weren't as funny as the laughs they provoked at the table. The scribes tried vainly to mute the laughs, with fists over mouths.

Least amused was Bowl president, Jim "Junkyard" Junker, who was discoursing from the podium on the many benefits senior citizens would derive from the game.

But the sotto-voce conversation continued at the press table.

"How about this," said the Albuquerque News. "How about a general award for the best bowl finish. It would go for the Best Climax of the Year. The sponsor? Viagra."

Junker scowled at the offending table and sat down. A bowl official came to the rescue. He gave a pre-arranged signal to the Southwestern marching band waiting in the wings. Immediately, it started snaking through the hall, blaring out the Rattlers' fight song, "Snakebit Forever."

The atmosphere surrounding the game was light-hearted. At one press conference, Devine and the Southern Cal coach, T.D. Powers, traded quips and threats, no malice intended or taken.

USC limited player interviews to 15 minutes at the end of each practice. Southwestern, on the other hand, had a more relaxed format. It made players available anytime, anywhere. The Rattlers, supposedly neophytes at public relations, lighted up for the press.

Previously unpublished and mostly untrue stories delighted the metro writers, who swallowed the manufactured hype with no doubts and no questions.

Linebacker Joe Fridena told of surviving a near-fatal childhood ailment. Tackle Michael Matuszak recalled his teenage rescue of a toddler from a nearby lake. Bill Bovine told of his spiritual communications with that great coach in the sky. Halfback Rashad Moshier captivated the media with a recitation of his rugged and dangerous early life in gang warfare in Watts.

"If not for football, I would by now likely be sitting in death row in some prison," he said.

Drawing the largest crowds was Australian Rod Norman. He recalled riding kangaroos barebacked as a kid. It prepared him, he said, for later wrestling matches with sharks off the great barrier reef.

So it went. And, in the jovial mood, the Fossils decided they should do something different to perk up the pre-game warmups, a ritual as exciting as watching paint dry or grass grow. Coaches are slaves to habit. Every pre-game warmup is the same. Punters punt. Passers pass. Offensive linemen bump one another. Defenders backpeddle to haul in soft passes launched by coaches with worn-out arms. Exciting stuff.

So, what to do different? Stumped, the coaches reacted as they usually do. They turn to the Sports Information Director, who had become athletic director.

"Hey, Bull," said Devine to me. "We want something different to juice up warmups. Got to give announcers something to talk about. You're in charge. Find something."

I started digging through old books for a clue. One of my favorites, for authentic college football history, is Tim Cohane's documentary on the great college football coaches of the twenties and thirties.

On page 146, I found what I wanted. Vanderbilt was playing Tennessee, winner of 20 straight games, in 1939. Vandy had lost five and was a huge underdog to the Vols.

Freddie Russell, respected sports editor of the Nashville Banner and a thoroughly-solid citizen, had this uncharacteristic whim. He took it to Vanderbilt coach Ray Morrison, who listened and laughed.

Russell nearly sold the idea but eventually Morrison nixed it.

"It was an extreme situation, calling for extreme measures," Russell recalled. "I wanted Morrison to come on to the field for the pre-game workout with a baseball fungo bat and his players dressed in baseball suits. How would it have affected the Tennessee players? And the coaches? I still wonder."

Wonder no more, Freddie. Southwestern grabbed your idea and ran with it.

Southwestern had upset Nebraska, Texas and Michigan but still was, in many minds, considered unworthy of facing Southern California, alias

Tailback U. And there was among the USC coaches and players a certain arrogance about playing this virtually unknown team from Phoenix. Southern Cal was rated No. 6, Southwestern No. 13.

It seemed to me that Russell's idea about appearing in baseball suits might rattle Trojan players. Or at least bring a smile to their complacent faces. I wondered?

The Fossils bought the idea. What the heck. In this instance, as in so many in this crazy, mixed-up season, they had nothing to lose. They would return to the anonymity of retirement, anyway.

They also bought another wild idea which had been perking in the active mind of Doug Weaver. An assistant under Devine at Missouri, Weaver coached at Kansas State and Southern Illinois and became athletic director at his alma mater, Michigan State.

Weaver's wild idea was to pump up a football with helium and use it in pre-game warmups to disconcert the opponent.

Fossils originally vetoed the idea as being too weird, even for them. But along came Jeff Van Raaphorst, quarterback of Arizona State's 1987 Rose Bowl champions.

"Not as weird as you might think, gentlemen," said Van Raaphorst, now a radio commentator. "When I was in high school, my coach tried the same thing. And in the warmup I was overthrowing my receivers by 30 yards."

So, an hour before kickoff in the Citrus Bowl, out came a Southwestern center, two punt returners and Rod Norman-all dressed in normal football attire. Not normal, however, were two footballs pumped up with helium.

Colleges these days have more information on an opponent than possibly can be devoured. USC had six films on the Rattlers, scouting reports from three schools and another from a scouting service.

Still, by habit, the USC special teams coach, Joe Clanahan, stood on the sideline, clutching two stop watches, timing the opposition punts. He was interested in two times-the time required from snap until the kicker's toe hit the football and the time the football stayed in the air. Time used to kick could determine if punts were blockable. Hang time, as it is called, also determined if the kick was returnable and how far back the punt receiver should stand.

Norman put toe to the helium-filled football quickly. Clanahan timed it, looked at his watch, and stuck it back in his pocked. He couldn't believe what he saw. He timed again. Same result. The clock showed 5 seconds plus a few tenths-considerably longer than scouting reports showed. Clanahan called over a colleague. He timed the hang time with similar results.

This wasn't disaster. USC might have to signal for more fair catches, and maybe move punt returners back 10 yards or so. But the fabulous punting exhibition was disconcerting. Doubts surfaced concerning the validity of scouting reports.

Not as disconcerting, however, was what happened next. Out came the rest of the players suited up in Southwestern baseball togs and gloves. Darryl Rogers took one group to a corner of the endzone, where they took makeshift infield practice. A pepper game started in the other corner. A pitcher warmed up on the 20-yard line, tossing to a player in full catcher's regalia.

USC players gawked. Some nudged others, and laughed. Others looked perplexed, confused. What the hell was this? Typical was tight end J. W. Tipsy. He was supposed to be in a line going out for soft passes thrown rather poorly by an assistant coach. Tipsy instead was looking at the baseball players. The ball struck him in the nose.

Coaches huddled. Was this a joke? Were they being needled? What would the press think? What would other coaches think? How would Southwestern use this equipment in the game? Was it legal to wear catcher's chest pads in the defensive line?

The coaches were at first puzzled, then befuddled and then angry. The game was being compromised, turned into a sideshow by these clowns. Were the Trojan coaches and players being embarrassed on national TV? What could they do?

Nothing. The baseball uniforms, and the players therein, left after 30 minutes. In their dressing room beneath the south stands, they changed into football uniforms and stretched strenuously to prepare physically.

They smiled. The stunt was successful. It put doubt in the Trojans' minds. It also took Trojan minds off the upcoming game. It served the purpose. Freddie Russell would have loved it.

CHAPTER 32

There are no secrets in football, we are told. That is because coaches can't keep a secret. They are big blabbermouths, especially when they have a new play or a new formation to brag about. They spout off to foe and friend alike.

It's an ego thing. Friends hear about the innovations first. Foes must wait until the subject is broached in trade magazines or at clinics.

It's one great profession of sharing.

Still, it seemed a tad strange when Arizona State coach Bruce Snyder shared his thoughts on trick plays so readily. After all, ASU and Southwestern were to meet for the first time the next season. Plus, the two schools compete for many of the same fans.

Before leaving Phoenix for the bowl, Kush and Devine, both legendary ASU coaches, visited Snyder in his ASU office-a beautiful launching pad designed to wow recruits. The south wall featured memorabilia. The north wall, all glass, overlooked Sun Devil stadium.

Snyder was not at all reluctant to share his secrets with Devine and Kush. If he could contribute to the Fossils' bag of dirty tricks, he was more than willing, particularly for this bowl game. Snyder's ulcer still kicked up when he thought of USC firing his buddy, John Robinson.

Snyder reached into a pile of video tapes and extracted one 30-minute tape full of nothing but trick plays.

"I just love trick plays," said Snyder, belaboring the obvious. "And I like them early. I think it does something psychologically to your own kids. I think you play looser, and with more abandon, if the players know you are not conservative.

"I believe you should use your trick play before the other guy uses his. I tell my staff I'll be mad at them if the other team runs one before we do. There's some logic in that. I believe the longer the game goes on the less likely you are to call a trick play. And if you're behind, the other team will be more alert to tricks."

With that, Snyder showed his tape. It should be preserved for, if not the Smithsonian, at least for the college football hall of fame. It was a collection of plays he had installed at California and Arizona State. Some he had never run in games, only in practice against his own defense. There must have been 20 variations of the wide receiver reverse. He had the reverse and the double reverse and the fake reverse and the pass off all of them.

The mouths of Devine and Kush dropped open. The Fossils were to use two of Snyder's plays against USC, which delighted Snyder.

Snyder's hit-em-quick trick-play philosophy already had been adopted by the Rattlers. Remember? They opened two games with onside kicks. The kick against Nebraska was successful. The kick against Washington State boomeranged into a Cougar touchdown.

Another onside kick for openers against Southern Cal was out of the question. Or was it?

Not after Mike Westhoff visited the Marriott headquarters of the Rattlers in Orlando. Westhoff is a grizzled veteran who, in 13 years as special teams coach for the Miami Dolphins, has become the guru of the onside kick.

Westhoff came to the Rattler camp to chew over old times with Kush, under whom he had served both with the Baltimore/Indianapolis team and a United States Football League club in Phoenix.

Westhoff was aware of the Rattlers' love affair with trick plays. Like Snyder, he was a serious collector of trick plays.

Mike was sharing a post-practice brew with Rattler coaches. "Probably the most popular trick now is our onside kick. A lot of people are using versions of it."

Kush's shoulders hunched in a shrug. "OK, Mike, what's so tricky about your onside kick...you do it or you don't do it, don't you?"

Mike grinned. He had been waiting for the invitation.

"Well, we've got the team record in the NFL for doing three onside kicks against New England in one game. And we recovered all three. The first kick was a surprise. The last two at the end of the game weren't. You can do this when everybody in the world knows what you are going to do. Or, you can use it as a surprise.

"The way we do it. it goes back to 1987. We've got that bare-footed kicker Tony Franklin for a short time. He taught me this kick. It requires a lot of athletic ability. Morton Anderson has done it very well.

"What you do is...first, you tee the ball fairly straight up. The kicker hits down on the ball, and drives it straight into the ground. The ball will bounce real high and come down about 10 or 12 yards down the field. The ball goes up so high you think maybe it's a center jump in basketball. First time we ran it against our own team, our receiver tried to fair catch it but you can't do that because the ball has hit the ground.

"Now, we have people designated to block two of the receiving team's up-front people, to clear a path for our guys assigned to recover the football. And you use tall guys, guys who played basketball, good rebounder types. These guys all can dunk. So you can imagine how high up they can go."

The more Westhoff talked about the kind of athletes needed, the more closely the Rattlers seemed to fit the requirements. Rod Norman was the kicker-athlete required. He could juggle a football on his cleated toes. And for a basketball player who can dunk, the Rattlers had 6–8 Muhammad Jones, who caught the alley oop endzone pass from another former basketball player, 6–4 Jose Garcia, against Michigan. These two were assigned as the good-hands folks to gather in the bouncing football long before it came to earth.

The play looked great in practice. It looked even better when the Rattlers used it to open the Citrus Bowl game against Southern Cal.

Norman drove the ball into the ground. It bounced 12 feet high and was just long enough to sail over the first wave of Trojan players. Fullback Bill Bovine and offensive tackle Michael Matuszak collaborated on cross blocks. Bovine blocked the Trojan in front of Matuszak and Matuszak blocked the player in front of Bovine.

It was like the parting of the Red Sea. Jones and Garcia bolted 12 yards through the gaping hole to where the football was expected to return to earth.

For Garcia and Jones, the assignment was too easy. They had a freeway through the first line of defenders. They arrived in time to camp under the high hopper. Either could have caught it. Jones caught it, then kidded the press afterwards.

"We got there so early we had a coin flip to decide who would make the catch," Garcia said. "Jones won the toss, so I had to get out of his way."

It was still necessary to convert the successful onside kick into a score. The Rattlers did it by digging back into the football archives.

We tend to think of trick plays as latter-day innovations. Wrong. In flipping through Tim Cohane's book about the outstanding coaches of the twenties and the thirties, I came across a devious device used by Chicago's legendary Amos Alonzo Stagg against Iowa in the mid twenties.

The play was beautiful because of its simplicity. It was almost like Lucy pulling the football back as Charlie Brown attempted a placekick.

The Chicago fullback pointed beyond the Iowa line and asked loudly, "What's that?" When the defense turned to see, the ball was snapped to the fullback, who burst free for a 20-yard gain.

Stagg, although a stickler on the rules, enjoyed injecting guile. He said, of the fullback trick, "Anyone who would fall for such a trick should be encouraged to."

I reported the Stagg trick to the Fossils, who opted to use a modern-day version on the first play from scrimmage, assuming the Rattlers could recover the opening onside kick, which they did.

Quarterback Bobby Joe Jackson was back in a shotgun formation. Fullback Bill Bovine went in motion right, stopped, looked beyond the USC defense, and asked loudly, "What's that?"

The Rattlers, by the book, had to stand stock still for one second before the ball was snapped. No problem. The Trojan defense was still looking the other way, trying to find what attracted Bovine's attention.

Ronald Owens, the walk-on sprinter from the track team, was stationed wide left. He ran a quick slant route. His defender was looking the other way. No one was within five yards of Owens. It seemed impossible to be so wide open so quickly, but remember, football players now can go nearly 40 yards in four seconds.

Bobby Joe Jackson's pass was fielded with no difficulty by the speeding Owens. John Ramsey, the right wide receiver, went deep and in. The speeding Owens cut behind him, and Ramsey, simply by standing still, screened off the Trojan safety. Owens was looking back over his shoulder as he crossed into the endzone. The play went 53 yards.

On the extra point attempt, the Rattlers lined up in a weird formation, borrowed from ASU. However, a lot of teams have used this gimmick. Most call it a "swinging gate." Oklahoma used it against Army as early as 1946. Penn State calls the same thing the "muddled huddle" and used it in the Fiesta Bowl.

In the swinging gate, the center, holder and kicker line up normally in front of the goal posts. But the rest of the team-six linemen and two backs-line up to the left of the kicker. If the defense does not move to cover those players isolated on the left, the ball is snapped wide left. Sounds difficult, but it isn't. The ball, instead of being snapped between the center's legs as it normally is, is instead tossed in front of the left leg. It becomes easy to spiral the football directly to a back stationed 5 to 10 yards left of the center. The surprise snap and the fact that the offensive team has an edge in numbers at the point of attack frequently leads to two points.

If the defense adjusts by moving its people, the kicking team simply shifts to a normal place-kicking formation and kicks.

Southern Cal, having faced the formation in playing ASU, knew how to adjust. The Rattlers shifted into a normal place-kick alignment and kicked the point. But Southwestern had established the swinging gate threat, which was to play a huge role later.

Sportswriters are forever trying to write parts of their story in their mind as the game unfolds. It's a good exercise, unless the writer becomes so wedded to his idea he won't discard it when the situation changes.

Scoop Simon was so endeared to his first thoughts that he hammered them out immediately on his computer. The thought had to be shelved later but his words, resurrected from the computer, accurately portrayed the feeling at the time. Scoop wrote:

"A football game can not be won on the opening kickoff. But this one came tantalizingly close to being decisive. The Rattlers successfully recovered an onside kick, despite the fact that USC expected such a kick and had practiced defending against such an eventuality.

"The psychological damage was significant. USC players were riled about Rattlers popping off to the media, rattled by the hang time of the helium punts and disturbed by Southwestern warming up in baseball uniforms.

"But the crowning blow was being outsmarted on the opening onside kick. USC Coaches told players daily to be wary of the Rattlers' onside kick. The squad had spent 15 minutes daily to prepare on defusing the onside kick they were sure would be used against them.

"The added work and warnings only made it more embarrassing for the Trojans when they were victimized before most of the patrons had opened their popcorn boxes.

"Southwestern was ahead 7–0 less than a minute into the game, when the Rattlers pulled out an old distraction play from the bag of tricks of legendary Amos Alonzo Stagg to complete a 53-yard touchdown pass."

CHAPTER 33

Back-to-back onside kicks? Unheard of. What happened the second time was not a true onside kick, but a fake onside kick, if such a football maneuver can be said to exist.

Prior to the kickoff, the Rattlers, in an unusual move, huddled on the 25-yard line, 10 yards behind where the football sat on a tee waiting to be kicked. The referee, his patience stretched by the extended huddle, warned the Rattlers to break it up or face a delay-of-game penalty.

Out of the huddle snaked the players, unfurling like a coiled rope. Seven of the Rattlers circled to the left of the kicker and three to their right. Alarmed, USC quickly adjusted to the strength, moving their troops to their right. Seemed reasonable. There's where the danger seemed to lurk. Matuszak and Bovine were both there.

Given a bit more time, the Trojans might have detected something unusual about the personnel right of the kicker. But the impatient referee signaled for the kickoff immediately.

To the right of kicker Rod Norman were three small, swift and elusive Rattlers. They were wide receiver John Ramsey, halfback Rashad Moshier and the former track sprinter Ronald Owens.

After the ball was kicked, the three weaved through token traffic with ease and speed. Norman, who had that flair for the spectacular, had been told only to toe one of his low screaming, bounding kickoffs toward the right corner.

Norman said that the ensuing kickoff was by design, a boot that he had worked out on his own. Doubtful. The football did, however, hop crazily down the field, like a ball in a pinball machine, until it reached the USC 30-yard line. There, for reasons no one will completely understand, it took one high hop. It could not have been by design. No toe is that educated.

Standing there awaiting for the descent of the football was Trojan Kent Young, who also returned punts for USC. As the ball descended so did the three swift Rattlers-Owens, Moshier and Ramsey.

It was disconcerting. Various frantic thoughts raced through Young's mind. The soaring ball and the opposition would arrive at about the same time. Young did what came natural for a punt returner. He stuck his right arm skyward, signaling for a fair catch.

He, instead, was fair game. Once the football bounces, and it had several times, a returner no longer can take refuge in the fair catch provision. At the last instant, Young realized his mistake. He stepped aside, letting the ball bounce.

That was a worse mistake. On a kickoff, the kicking team recovering a kick after it travels at least 10 yards gains possession. Owens recovered on the 19-yard line.

From a USC standpoint, this was the worst start since the Bay of Pigs. It got worse.

In the wake of the recovered kickoff, platoons shuttled in from both sides of the field. Hastily, the Rattlers got their offensive team assembled and into the ball game. They had, as prescribed, 11 players on the field, when Bobby Joe Jackson lined up in a shotgun formation. Suddenly, from the Rattler sideline came some serious shouting.

"You got 12 people in there. Get Jones out of there. You want a penalty. Jones…Jones…get your ass out of there before it costs us."

So off at full speed ran Jones Keith. There actually were only 11 players on the field, including Jones, who took special care to run laterally. When he got 10 yards from the sideline, he stopped and turned toward the huddle. His extended forefinger counted off the players …nine, ten, eleven.

"Only 11 players," he announced, thus satisfying a rule that a team may not deceive a foe in this manner. But, with the needed one second pause, the ball was snapped. Keith turned and sped down the sidelines. Jackson lobbed the 19-yard pass to him in the endzone. Easy catch. Touchdown.

Only 1:32 had elapsed and Southwestern had two touchdowns. The extra point again was added after the Rattlers shifted out of their swinging gate formation into a normal place-kicking alignment.

In looking back, it was too easy, too quick. Had it been baseball, the touchdowns would have been ruled as unearned. Had it been boxing, the fight would have ended as a technical knockout.

Those 14 points loomed large on the scoreboard, The Rattlers may have become complacent, losing a bit of their mental edge.

They were like the guy who walked across Niagara Falls on a tight rope with a python wrapped around his neck. What could they do for an encore?

Contrary to the story which had been writing itself in Scoop Simon's mind, the Trojans were not befuddled nor bedazzled. They were, most of all, angered. A new resolve grew in their innards.

Southern Cal answered the trickery with sheer, raw power. The basis for the Trojans dominance during the coaching stint of John McKay and the early days of John Robinson was the tailback sweep. The Trojans swept left and then right.

Student body left, student body right. That's how it looked anyway. The pattern varied slightly. The ball could be pitched or handed to the tailback. It could be run from the I formation, or split backs or, most often, from a power I. The Trojans at times had as many as four players blocking for the tailback—two backs and two pulling guards.

McKay, in the days of the student body sweeps, was blessed with superior tailbacks like O. J. Simpson and Marcus Allen. Tailback U., they called Southern Cal. And the tailbacks were all great athletes. The more they ran, the better they were. General laws governing fatigue hold that players used too often become weary. But not the USC tailbacks. They seemed stronger on their 30th carry than their first.

Questioned about overworking his tailbacks, McKay once said: "Is there a tailback union? The football is not very heavy."

The sweep was awesome stuff. Well-heeled alums yearned for a return to the old days when the tailbacks terrorized foes. and they lobbied for same.

The three weeks of workouts prior to a bowl are one of the huge fringe benefits that go with post-season bids. That interval is an ideal time to experiment, to add new wrinkles, to try untested players. USC used that time well to install and refine those sweeps that had once been the school's meal tickets. If nothing else, the sweeps would be a good changeup to the West-Coast offense on which the Trojans now relied. Relied too much, probably.

Return of the USC sweep in the Citrus Bowl left Rattlers awed. They didn't know whether it was a rerun of a subway rush or a leftover from a Cecil B. DeMille flick.

Southern Cal had the USC type tailback waiting in the wings to be recognized. Roosevelt Eger, a freshman, was big and he was swift. On this day, however, all he needed was to get behind his posse of blockers and run.

USC, proving it was unshaken by the 14–0 deficit, unveiled the revival of the sweep on the next possession, marching 74 yards in eight plays, six of the carries were sweeps featuring Eger. The point was kicked and the margin reduced to seven.

There was one obvious answer to the bulldozer tactics, that is, not let the Trojans have the football. The Rattlers decided to fall back on a ball-possession game, safe, short yardage with high percentage plays. One problem. The Rattlers had thrived on their trick plays. They did not have the muscle to out-muscle USC.

On its next possession, Southwestern managed only one first down, kicked and set the USC juggernaut in motion again from its 30-yard line. Eger ran right for 10, left for eight and the fullback, Leon Crossfield, slashed up the middle for six on a trap play.

Eger ran left for 12, then in a new twist, faked to the right where all his blockers were headed, and countered back over left guard. It was good for only five yards but, as coaches' say, it kept the defense honest.

Eger then fell back on a McKay staple, the off-tackle play. Conditioned as they were to the sweep, the Rattlers were caught unawares. Eger shook off a linebacker and scored from 29 yards out.

The extra point tied the score, 14–14, with 8:49 remaining in the first half.

The Rattlers held on for dear life. Only an interception, when Eger threw short on the sweep pass, and a fumbled punt kept Southwestern in the game.

CHAPTER 34

Rarely, probably never, has the halftime of a tied game been so grim. Southwestern felt as if it was on life support despite the 14–14 deadlock. Someone should have piped the funeral march into the Rattler dressing room. Some Southwestern players sat with towels draped over their heads, looking at the floor. Joe Fridena kicked his helmet. It would have been good for three points from 30 yards. Others had hands steepled in prayer. There was nary a smile, a joke, or a promise of better things in the second half.

Coaches gathered, as they usually do, in an outside hall, to discuss what topics the position coaches would take up with their charges.

"Just what in hell can we do to stop the sweep, Al?" Devine asked Onofrio. It was ironic. The sweep was causing their headaches now. During their 13 years at Missouri, the Tigers' sweep had given others headaches.

Onofrio shook his head sadly. "We've tried everything."

The Rattler defensive repertoire had grown with each game. The seven diamond remained the mainstay, and little nuances had been added to shift to or away from the short side of the field, and to slant linemen in either direction. The Rattlers had three different alignments to use with their three-deep secondary, and could go to a four-deep alignment.

By and large, the defense had held up well except against Texas. A system was devised after that to move in and out of defenses just as the ball was snapped.

"The thing is our seven diamond should work well against the sweep," Onofrio said. "I think we have to just do what we're doing but do it better."

Jack Mitchell, although he had helped develop a wishbone quarterback, was assigned to the defensive secondary.

"There's one thing I'd like to try, Al," Mitchell said. "You'll remember our Kansas team had some luck against the Missouri sweep in 1960."

Al remembered, too well. Mitchell's Kansas team handed Missouri its only defeat of the season, 23–7, at Columbia. The result still is listed in the Missouri press guide but with an asterisk indicating Kansas had to forfeit the game because of using an ineligible player.

"In that one, we had some luck in trying to push the sweep to the sideline rather than trying to just contain it," Mitchell said. "It would take some time to put in that defense. But I think if you let me talk to the outside guys we can use a little of that theory against Southern Cal."

It was worth a shot. So into a small isolated area, Mitchell took the cornerbacks, the safeties and two men on the end of the defensive line.

"This goes back years ago to when I was an assistant at Texas Tech," Mitchell told his players. The players shrugged. They wanted something for now, not posterity.

"There was this old retired coach who hung around at all the practices. One day he told me, 'You guys on defense never use Sammy Sideline. You've got to use the sideline. That's the best thing going for you on defense, that sideline.'"

The players looked at each and smiled. Sammy Sideline?

Safety James Killingsworth nudged the guy next to him, and said in a stage whisper, "What we need is Tommy Touchdown."

Mitchell continued as if he had not heard the comment. "There's a lot to that sideline thing. The sideline is in there every play. It's never blocked. It's never hurt. But we aren't using it.

"You guys aren't getting beat by the sweep. You're getting beat by the cut back on the sweep. We play contain. The cornerback tries to contain, push the carrier to his inside.

"This half, we'll do it the other way. I want the cornerback, the safety, and you two outside linemen…all of you, to force the tailback into the sidelines and make damn sure you don't leave any alleys or tunnels where he can cut back. Make sure, whatever you do, to force him to the sideline."

It might be stretching it to give Sammy Sideline a game ball. But the changeup helped. It at least gave players hope and something else to think about. And it gave Roosevelt Eger a different look to contend with.

On the first scrimmage play of the second half, Eger circled right and started looking for places to cut back. There were the linemen, hand-fighting with the pulling guards. Their thrust was to the outside. Had Eger cut back, he would be in their hands. The same picture presented itself as Eger reached the Rattler safety and then the cornerback. He ended up running out of bounds for a minus two yards.

Eger wasn't stopped by Sammy Sideline, but he was slowed. The aura of invincibility demonstrated in the first half faded away with his repeated trips out of bounds. For the first half, he had gained 125 yards on 17 carries. In the second half, he picked up 47 yards on 16 carries.

That, in itself, should have swung the tide for Southwestern. But the Rattlers couldn't get anything going either. A part of it was injuries. Quarterback Bobby Joe Jackson injured his shoulder in the first half.. Matuszak, the standout at offensive tackle, was hobbling on a strained knee ligament pull. Halfback Rashad Moshier got a concussion after being blindsided on the opening kickoff of the second half.

Southwest didn't give up on trick plays. Far from it. They ran the single wing and the wishbone. The buck lateral and the pitchout. They tried the punt-run option by Norman. They even tried the Joe Kapp play, where a pass from the short man in punt formation was supposed to resemble a punt. USC refused to bite.

It was revealed afterward that USC Coach T. D. Powers had spent the half-time lecturing on trick plays.

"Stay at home," he pleaded. "I don't care where the motion is going, or where a player looks or points. I want you to stay in your assigned spot even if a tornado hits. Stop only for the ref's whistle, and be danged sure about that."

Good advice, that. As the fourth period started, the Rattlers pulled a wide-receiver reverse pass. Normally, the safety will come up to stop the reverse. But the USC safety, A. J. First, heeded his coach's words. He stayed deep. Sure enough, John Ramsey showed up in his area. The other wide receiver, Jones Keith, had taken the reverse and was to launch the pass.

The wobbly, high toss was short. Ramsey could not reverse directions quickly enough. Facing the passer, First broke quickly on the ball, intercepted and returned 22 yards to the Southwestern 19-yard line.

From there, in four-down country, USC relied on power football. Roosevelt Eger bolted off tackle for six hard yards. A counter by the fullback, Leon Crossfield, added five more. First down on the eight-yard line. Eger on the trap play up the middle and then on a sweep left put the ball on the one, from where quarterback Jose Armijo sneaked in.

Cheerleaders and bands have never won a football game, except maybe for a trombone player's block in that Stanford-California multi-lateral game of 1982. Remember. Down with only four seconds left, California resorted to a sandlot play. They made five laterals. The final recipient of a lateral sped into the endzone, knocking down a trombone player.

And here, at the Citrus Bowl, cheerleaders were front row center when an extra point attempt was blocked by a flying cheerleader. It provided the needed mental lift.

Charlie Chang and Dennis Wong, a pair of gymnasts and martial arts experts turned cheerleaders, had come to Devine a week before the game with an unusual proposal. They claimed they could block place kicks more than 60 per cent of the time.

Gymnasts, they insisted, could be valuable on the football field. They cited the winning touchdown scored by Arizona quarterback Ortege Jenkins against Washington. Ortege was faced with three defenders lined up at the two yard line. Ortege simply did a full flip over the trio and came down on his feet in the endzone.

Chang and Wong had developed a routine to celebrate each Rattler score. Chang, his back turned toward the playing field, formed a stirrup with his hands. Wong ran toward his cohort and stuck his right foot in the stirrup. His momentum with an added lift from Change shot Wong into the air. He did a full flip, coming to the turf about at the point the football leaves the kicker's foot.

Just for kicks, so to speak, the pair started trying to time the flip to coincide with place kicks on the field. It was not as difficult as one might imagine. If the climbing football got on the same trajectory going up as did Wong coming down, there was a reasonable period in which the two might collide.

Wong and Chang had enlisted the aid of an intramural touch football kicker to work out the timing. They may have exaggerated in estimating a 60 percent success rate, but they were able to connect at least 40 per cent of the time.

Why not, Devine asked himself. His team had beaten Michigan when linebacker Bob Crable stepped on a teammate's back and leaped to block a field coach.

This was no more far-fetched than that, or, as a matter of fact, some of the other things the Rattlers had tried. This particular moment seemed the appropriate time to try the human scud missile. USC led 20–14 with 9:51 remaining.

The obviously undersized gymnasts attracted little attention until they went on the field as USC lined up for the extra point try. Then, Wong and Chang, stationed behind the Southwestern line, took their Karate stance, arms extended as if to chop one another and started shouting those guttural, loud words associated with the art.

The USC holder, Tim Wright, stood up, looking over at the uproar. Then the rest of team arose to determine the cause of the strange interruption.

And T. D. Powers, the USC coach, started to run onto the field but was restrained by his assistants. Powers settled for calling a timeout and desperately waving the referee over to the sidelines.

"They can't do that," stormed Powers. "It jams our snap count."

That ignored the fact that the holder uses hand signals to call for the ball.

"If you can yell out signal changes, I see no reason the defense can't yell out its instructions," said referee Zack Brazil.

So, the teams lined up again. Again Chang and Wong had their shouting match. But as the ball was snapped, Wong spurted forward, planted his foot in Chang's hands and catapulted into the air, did his full flip, and descended like a swan coming in for a landing. He was directly in the path of the ascending kicked football. Wong's body was encased, beneath the jersey, in protective padding. It wasn't needed. His hand tipped the kick, sending it off course.

This time the assistants could not restrain Powers from coming on the field. The referee waved him off, nodding his head as if he understood.

And he did. The rules, changed after the same catapult block was used in a division III game, now provided that a teammate could not assist in the blocking of a place kick in such a manner.

So, the re-kick. This time, undisturbed by flying bodies, the boot was true. USC led 21–14 with 9:51 remaining.

But the tenor of the game had changed. The Rattlers were relaxed and/or inspired by the shenanigans. Their mental outlook was improved.

The Trojans, presuming perhaps that their superiority had been established, were content to sit on the lead. The desperate Rattlers tried everything in the play book. And some that were not. Devine actually scratched out one pass play in the sideline dirt, sandlot style. It didn't work.

With two minutes left, the Rattlers finally were able to manufacture a legitimate threat. It took guts. The reverse pass earlier had resulted in the game's key interception. But, digging deeper into the bag of trick plays, the Rattlers called a weird play from the video of ASU Coach Bruce Snyder.

"The Copper pass, we call it," Snyder had told Kush and Devine. "That's because we first ran it against California in the Copper bowl. It's reverse action with a flea flicker motion."

Gulp. This was a turnover about to happen.

Garcia took the snap from center and tossed to tailback Tim Pruitt running to his right. Then, the reverse. Wide receiver Jones Keith, running to his left, was slipped the ball by Pruitt. Meanwhile, quarterback

Garcia had dropped back about 10 yards, seemingly a spectator. But as Keith drew even with Garcia, he flipped the ball back to the quarterback.

"You'll get a line rush one way and then the other," Snyder had told the Southwestern coaches. "There's no way you can buy that amount of time on a straight dropback pass."

Pruitt, after handing off to the wide receiver, had circled deep and set up camp in the middle of the field, fully 10 yards beyond the nearest defender, Safety Jerome Morrissey.

As Garcia cocked his arm to pass, Morrissey socked himself in the helmet. "Geez, I stayed home but stayed home not deep enough."

Remember, Garcia was not a passer. He was a wishbone quarterback. His long, lofted pass fell short. But in so doing, it hit Morrissey in the back of the helmet. The back judge ruled the USC safety was face guarding, and called pass interference on him.

The 15-yard penalty advanced the ball to the 35-yard line.

Twice Garcia, on a fake keeper play off the Wishbone, used a chest pass to hit his towering tight end and basketball teammate, Muhammad Jones, with passes for 10 and 13 yards. Time was becoming a problem. Only 52 seconds remained and the ball was on the 12-yard line.

Another pass was needed. So pass Garcia did-the same chest pass, with the alley-oop arc, to the same Jones. The Trojans were ready for it. Powers had sent in his biggest linebacker, Robert Tilley, 6–4 and 240, with special instructions.

"Damn it, Tilley, I don't want you to get beat again by an oversized exile from the basketball team. You get on Jones. Don't let him get out. Throw your weight around. Block him, nudge him, do whatever you have to do to keep him from getting out."

Garcia, for a fledgling quarterback, had a lot of savvy. He saw Tilley was all over his 6–8 end, trying to keep him from becoming a receiver. Garcia threw anyway. The ball fell to the ground. But so did the umpire's flag. As a result of his one-sided wrestling match with Jones, Tilley was charged with pass interference.

The ball was moved to the six. Devine sent in a weird play, the same inside screen pass Jack Mitchell had used against him more than three decades earlier. A more unlikely play you'll never see. But the Trojans bit. Their lineman bolted through, intent on mayhem. The short toss to half-back Tim Pruitt found him with a six-man Rattler escort, and only two men to block. Touchdown, with two seconds left.

It was 21–20. Conventional wisdom called for kicking the tying extra point and settling for an extra period.

But Devine had one of his hunches. He called time out and called his coaches around him.

"Men, I'd like to roll the dice on this one," he said. "I'd like to run that pass Snyder showed us from the swinging gate. I know 99 of 100 coaches would kick it to get into overtime but we've been damned lucky to stay in this game, particularly with as many injuries as we've got. I'm willing to put it all on the line on one play if you are."

Darryl Rogers answered for the assistants. "Coach, I've had some experience with ties. The public will never hold it against you if you lose while going all out for a win. I say let's go for two."

So it was, that the Rattlers lined up in the swinging gate. In front of the goal post were fullback Bill Bovine, who snapped on place kicks; Garcia, who was to hold for the extra point, and Joe Don Hentzen, who was to kick. Off to their left, separated by five yards, was the rest of the team, were six linemen and two backs. Southern Cal may have relaxed a bit. After all, from this same formation Southwestern had shifted and kicked on the previous two conversions.

Instead, Bovine snapped to Garcia, who stood up. He rolled right. Hentzen, who couldn't block his little sister, led him. Up zoomed the only defensive back on that side of the field, homing in on Garcia. Just as he arrived, Garcia launched that now-familiar chest lob pass to Bovine. He caught it.

The referee's hands shot upward. Two points. Southwestern had scored and won, 22–21.

But Powers was not ready to accept that. You could almost see smoke coming out of his ears as he rushed onto the field to brace the referee, Zack Brazil.

"What the hell is going on," he demanded. "Anybody with a lick of sense knows you can't pass to the center."

Brazil shrugged. "He may have been a snapper, but he was an end because he was at the end of the line."

"But what about the number?" ranted Powers. "He didn't have the right number. He was an ineligible receiver."

Said Brazil in a calm voice. "He wore number 44. That's an eligible number. Case closed"

The USC president and team captain escorted Powers off the field. He was still ranting, his face as red as the Florida sunset.

A temporary stage was set up at midfield. Devine sent Joe Fridena up to collect the trophy. Garcia picked up more hardware as the Most Valuable Player.

The dressing room was bedlam. A few victory cigars showed up. Fortunately, the players used some tact. The champagne was served in Seven Up bottles.

It was 45 minutes after the game. The stands had emptied of all but a few venders and sweepers. But there sat Jo Devine, all alone in her wheelchair in the handicapped section.

The bowl official assigned to pick her up was swept up in the celebration and forgot Jo.

She sat there deserted but satisfied, smiling and filled with an inner warmth. She checked the scoreboard every so often. It was unchanged. Southwestern 22, Southern California 21.

That game, and others, were re-run in her mind. The one she thought of so often was Notre Dame's heartbreaking loss to Southern Cal, 17–13, in 1976.

How ironic, she thought. The Irish lost that one because of two pass interference calls on Luther Bradley. Here on this splendid Florida afternoon, they had beaten Southern Cal with the help of two pass interference calls. Maybe, she thought, it's like they say. Maybe all those calls even out in the long run.

Joe Fridena, after looking over most of the deserted stadium, found Jo, once again the forgotten football wife. Under his arm, Joe carried a football.

Joe was slightly embarrassed. He stuck the football at Jo and said, "Here, take this game ball, m'am...the guys wanted you to have it."

EPILOGUE

And all lived happily ever after.

True? Mostly.

The Fossils took great pains—and great pleasure in—selecting their choice for the next football coach at Southwestern State. They had been assigned only to ratify the choice of a committee, but the Fossils became their own committee and did all the searching. Each of the six called friends in the business, amassing a data base probably unmatched in any previous coaching search. President Justin White was delighted. The was the kind of buck college presidents like to pass along.

So where did the Fossils' far-flung search lead? This is the amusing part. It led only a few miles south to downtown Phoenix where Danny White was coaching the city's Arena Football League team.

The arena team, like Southwestern, was nick-named the Rattlers. It was suggested, by one newspaper wag, that the Fossils picked White only because he already had the rattlesnake embroidered on his coaching togs. Another suggested Danny's last name appealed to Southwestern president, Dr. Justin White.

There were more important things in Danny's favor. He was a Valley of the Sun hero. Maybe the biggest player ever. He had been a standout at

Mesa Westwood high school. ASU prospered under his quarterbacking, winning 32 of 36 games including three Fiesta Bowls.

The Fossils' final screening of its top 25 candidates was an arduous and tedious task. The wheel spinning ceased when Frank Kush arose and announced he wanted to stick in a plug for one of his old players, obviously Danny White.

"If we make him a head coach, Danny will be criticized for his lack of experience but believe me, Danny White would be fantastic. He has such a great understanding of offense. To me, he potentially is one of the best coaches I've ever been affiliated with. And he got a helluva lot of experience under Tom Landry."

White spent 13 years with Landry's Dallas Cowboys. the first four as understudy to Roger Staubach.

He took heat, as would any quarterback following the legendary Staubach, especially when Cowboy talent was slipping. He kept his chin up and took the team to two Super Bowls.

The Fossils listened to Kush sing his protege's praises and nodded to one another. They obviously supported Kush's conclusions. Motion passed, by unanimous nods.

The Fossils formally presented their recommendation two months after the season ended to President White. He was wowed by how deeply and painstakingly thorough the search had been. And became even more so.

The Fossils report was two pages, one a concise biography and the second a neat one-page summary of Danny White's plusses and minuses. Each category was graded on a basis of one to 10. Listed on the plus side were human relations, sub divided into player, media and public. There were grades on offense and defense, character and personality, innovation and adaptability.

In summary, White was given bad grades only in coaching experience and recruiting. Each was accompanied with an asterisk. In the footnotes, testimonials to Danny's coaching skills were included from Tom Landry and Roger Staubach. Kush attested to his former player's "unlimited potential" as a recruiter.

White's grade total was 104 of a possible 140.

"So how did you come up with so many exact figures on such subjective topics?" asked Dr. White.

Said Devine: "These are not just our personal opinions, sir. We all have good contacts in every coaching situation. Each report card is a summation of the private opinions of at least 25 experts who have had close contact with the coach."

"And how many prospects did you grade?"

Devine smiled. He had hoped to be asked. "We have with us, sir, 25 reports similar in depth to the one you now hold on Danny. And on a computer disk, we have in-depth raw data on 75 more coaches."

"And the grades on the others?"

"Well, we had one come in at 109 and another at 107. But we felt the intangibles made Danny the logical choice. On those intangibles, I'd like to ask Bull Bullington, our interim athletic director. No one knows the Valley better. He's been around for years as a sports columnist and then as a sports information director."

"Danny White has amazing, perhaps unparalleled drawing power in this community," I said. "His arena team packed America West arena for virtually every home game, twice winning the league championship.

"And there's another fringe benefit in hiring Danny. Face it sir, Southwestern more and more will have to compete with Arizona State University for the entertainment dollar. Big Sun Devil donors long have been upset with ASU for never hiring ASU grads as assistants. Indeed, that has become a factor in recruiting.

"Rival recruiters keep pointing out to prospects, particularly those inclined toward coaching, that ASU did not think enough of its products to hire them as assistants".

So, on this very day, President Justin White assured the Fossils that Danny White, 46, who had never coached 11-man football, would be the Southwestern head coach.

The announcement was made the next day. Dr. White added his own post script, which was a surprise to all the Fossils except one.

"We have another surprise announcement at this time," he told the media in attendance. "On my own, without aid of the Fossils, I have picked my own athletic director.

"He is Darryl Rogers, the youngest of the Fossils at 64. He has agreed to serve as athletic director for two years. We feel his experience as an athletic director plus his experience at recruiting and coaching at this level will provide Coach White a resource for consultation.

"But let it be clearly understood that Coach White is in charge of the football team. It will be his decision, and his alone, when he consults with Rogers."

President White was proud of the Fossils' hiring process, and considered it something of a coup. He had come up with a good choice, based on experts' opinion and evaluations. He was in an excellent fallback position. If Danny did not work out, the Fossils could be blamed. If he became a hero, the president could take his bows.

Also avoided was the embarrassing situations which so often arise during coaching searches as rumors run rampant.

The coach walks a public relations tight rope in changing jobs. The school wants him to be silent and his media friends want answers.

Only safe answer is that old standby, "no comment." But in most situations that is tantamount to admitting something is up.

Yet, it was no problem for the Fossils in their search. They said "no comment" to every question.

President White bragged to his friends about the Fossils' unique way of conducting the search. The old coaches showed diligence in methodically collecting data on prospects. That, plus the guaranteed privacy made it an ideal way to go, the president told his colleagues.

Which was a nice way for President White to pat his own back and still retain a semblance of humility.

So it was that the Fossils, in finding a job for Danny White, also found a job for themselves. Other institutions, also interested in a quick, private and methodical coaching search conducted by experts came to the Fossils pleading for help.

Born was a new enterprise, which came to be known as "Headhunters Confidential." It involved all the Fossils. Me too. As a publicity man, I was useless because the Fossils did not want publicity. But I was able to put the data and biographies together in a concise, professional manner. Besides, with me as the errand boy, the Fossils could get back to the golf course and rocking chairs more quickly.

Confidentiality was a major part of the process. Coaches could express interest in a move without it becoming public. Colleges could keep searches a secret.

Headhunters Confidential was a fount of information for both the institutions and the coaches. Using all their contacts in the business, the Headhunters were able to rate colleges on a 1 to 10 basis, as they had coaches, on factors important to coaches: Facilities, television show possibilities, shoe contracts, tutoring services, salary level for the coach and his aides and probable alum help.

Secrecy could be carried one more step, if needed. Taped interviews with college officials or with prospects could be made available with no names mentioned.

• • •

Shirley Tate and I got together probably once a week to discuss athletic department business. A few times, after a victory or a few drinks too many, we had indulged in some mild necking. There was only one time a kiss held the promise of more.

But I never dreamed there could be more. What would a younger, prettier and more intelligent woman see in an overweight, overaged ink-stained ragamuffin like me?

On the night of the bowl victory, I went with Shirley to a celebration party. We wound up in her hotel room for a nightcap.

Our parting kiss was only a peck. But as we stood there looking at one another, she draped her arms around my neck and delivered a harder, more juicy kiss.

That surprised me, but not as much as what followed.

"If this is headed where I think it is," she said, "I'm going to need some protection."

Gulp. Did I hear what I thought I heard?

"God, I haven't had one of those things since I was in high school," I said. "I wouldn't even know where to find them."

Shirley smiled at my embarrassment. "Well, down the road about a mile is an all-night Safeway.

"Safeway," she said. "Rather appropriate, wouldn't you say?"

So, to the Safeway the two of us went, parking our rented Taurus in front of the store. I was eager but reluctant at the same time. The embarrassment of checking out with a package of...well, those things... left my face red and my throat dry.

"Tell you what," I said. "If they don't have a man on the checkout stand, I'm not going to get those things. I just couldn't get up my nerve to buy…well, those things…from a woman."

Both checkout counters were manned by women. I picked up a quart of milk and a carton of orange juice and a pack of Trojans, which I tried to hide between the other two items on the conveyor belt. Trojans? Also appropriate on this particular day.

The nice young lady ran the items over the scanner, gave me my change and said with a pleasant smile, "Have a good evening."

And so we did. Many, many good evenings, especially on the honeymoon.